LUCID

ROBERT J. L. KUN

DEDICATION

This book is dedicated to my Family:

To my parents, for always loving and supporting me, and for raising me in a manner that allows me to truly believe I can do anything.

To my wife and son, for loving me despite having to suffer through my seemingly endless artistic pursuits and all of the frustrations that I emphatically vocalize throughout the process.

CONTENTS

ACKNOWLEDGMENTS

A special, *Thank you*, to all of my family and friends who have supported and encouraged me in the creation of this work.

A special, *Fuck you*, to all the naysayers who have told me throughout my life that I can't do it.

1 What's the Real World?

Aiden left midmorning. He swung by the drive-through for a biscuit and coffee and then settled in for the long ride ahead. Instead of cutting straight through town, he took the long way along the bay. The sunlight danced on the choppy waters as a pelican perched on a pier piling with its wings outstretched, drying them in the sun. The cool air whistled into the car through the slightly open windows. Seaweed filled the air with its thick, salty smell. As he saw the bridge in the distance, he noticed it was very tall and that the grade of the bridge looked excessively steep. He gripped the wheel little more tightly as he got closer. An uneasy feeling crept up in his stomach, the kind of feeling you get before you take a final exam, or before the starter's gun goes off at the beginning of a race... kind of like butterflies, but stronger. When he reached the base of the bridge, he thought to himself, *"This is ridiculous! Why would they make a bridge like this? It looks dangerous!"* The uneasy feeling quickly grew into fear. He tried to comfort himself,

"Everyone else seems to be getting across just fine, why should it be any different for me?" He pressed on the gas a little more to try to maintain his speed. The bridge got steeper, and steeper until the car could no longer climb it. Fear grew into panic. The tires began to spin, the car lost its momentum and then started sliding backwards. Careening out of control down the steep bridge, Aiden screamed.

Aiden lay in his bed, heart pounding and dripping with sweat. He ran his fingers through his long, thick, brown, curly hair and then rubbed his face. This wasn't the first time he had this dream and it seemed to be occurring more and more frequently. The nightmares started about six months ago, the insomnia, a few weeks after that. This double-edged sword was beginning to wear on him. If he could choose, he would take the nightmares, because once he was awake, the suffering was over, but when you don't sleep at night, the suffering lasts all of the next day long. Going to work on two- or three-hours sleep was miserable. It was hard to concentrate and the day seemed to drag on. People at work would always ask him if he was okay and offer advice on how he could get more sleep. He had already tried everything they suggested and none of it seemed to help. Aiden had thought that maybe his insomnia stemmed from the fear of having bad dreams. *"If I don't sleep, I can't have nightmares. Seems reasonable to me."* Why he started having the bad dreams was still a mystery. Trying to encourage himself to start the day, he said out loud, "Well, at least I slept last night. I've made it through worst days; I'll make it through this one." He dragged himself out of bed and slipped off his pajamas, an old T-shirt and a pair of boxers. He looked at himself in the mirror, forced a big smile, and flexed in the typical muscleman pose. "Let's go get some dude!" He was tall and slender, with a wiry, muscular build. At 27 years old, he didn't have to try that hard to look good. Eating healthy, lifting weights three times a week, and an active lifestyle was all it took. After a typical morning routine, he was out the door and headed off to work.

Aiden lived with Amy, his girlfriend, but Amy was already long gone. She worked at the zoo and had to be there at 6 o'clock in the morning in order to take care of the animals before the park opened at nine. The two of them had been living together for about a year and were quite happy together. It was their love of nature that brought them together. Aiden worked for the National Parks Department doing survey and CAD work. He made maps, drew up plans for park improvements, and worked out in the field doing surveys of the parks in the area. One of his favorite jobs was looking at photos from game cameras that had been placed throughout the parks and mapping the various types of wildlife that the cameras picked up. Sometimes, if things were slow, Aiden would work with the field crews doing park maintenance. That's how he and Amy met. Aiden was working on a hiking trail, repairing damage by a recent storm. As he was shoveling stone onto a section of a trail that had been washed away, he noticed a young lady looking at him. She had long, straight, natural red hair, fair skin, and a smattering of freckles on her cheeks and nose. Her long, lean frame was complemented by her gentle curves. She was taking a water break with her friends, sitting upon a large rock and basking in the sunlight that snuck through the trees. When their eyes met, she gave Aiden a smile, which he returned. He walked over to her and introduced himself,

"Hi, I'm Aiden. I hope you're enjoying your time in the forest today."

"Why yes I am Aiden," She replied, "I'm Amy, a pleasure to meet you."

They shook hands with a joking sense of formality. The next night, they were on their first date.

There was a bookstore on the way home from Aiden's work, so he decided to stop by and see if he could find a book about dreams. Yes, he could search the web for the same information, but he preferred books. Books were better for a number of reasons: 1) Books have been written by real authors and gone through whatever the process is to be published, instantly giving them more credibility than anything you can find on line. 2) Aiden looked at a computer screen enough at work, so a book was a nice change of pace. 3) You can bring a book with you anywhere, without the need for a computer, or a power source, or a Wi-Fi connection. You can throw one in your backpack, go for a hike, and read it in the middle of the woods. 4) Books often have a unique air about them; whether they are old and musty or freshly printed and reeking of ink. Aiden liked making that extra connection with a book by using his sense of smell. (Aiden smelled everything: books, clothes, electronic equipment, plants, chemicals, suitcases that had been in the attic awhile, whatever that sticky stuff was on the counter...everything. Amy often called him her bloodhound). Another bonus of going to the bookstore was there was a girl who worked there that Aiden kind of liked. She had a look that was part nerd and part punk that worked really well for her. She was friendly, sarcastic and standoffish all at once. Aiden asked her for help and she led him to the section where all the books about dreams were located.

"Having some problems at night?" she asked with a little dig in her tone.

"You could say that."

With that she turned and walked away and Aiden began his search through the handful of books on the subject. He narrowed it down to two books, but had trouble deciding which one was best, so he brought them over to the girl at the store.

"Which one do you think I should get?"

After briefly inspecting the two books, she said, "Definitely this one."

"How did you decide so quickly?"

"Because this one is more expensive and I've got an ESOP plan at the store," she said with a smirk, suggesting she was joking, but then continued to ring up the more expensive book just the same.

By the time Aiden got home, Amy had already taken a shower, changed into fresh clothes, and started working on dinner. She stood at the kitchen counter cutting vegetables, her wet hair still wrapped in a towel.

"Where you been sweetie?" Amy said with a friendly tone.

"I stopped by the bookstore on the way home,"

"Did you get anything?"

"Well, I've been thinking about my bad dreams and how I've not been sleeping well, so I decided to get a book that could maybe help me out" Aiden said sheepishly, hoping Amy would not poke fun.

Amy walked over to him and kissed him on the cheek. "Well, I hope it helps you. I know you've been struggling for quite some time and it must be very difficult. You know, if there's anything I can do to help you, I will."

Why Aiden thought she would make fun of him, he didn't know, because Amy was always supportive of him and sensitive to his problems. Aiden embraced Amy, and held her in his arms for a while. With a pat on the butt and a kiss on her forehead he said,"...and *THAT* is why you are the best!"

Over dinner, they discussed their plans for the evening.

"I was thinking of just reading tonight and then turning in early in hopes of catching up on some sleep" Aiden said.

With a tentative tone, Amy suggested, "Well, if it's not going to bother you, I was going to ask Zoe if she wanted to come over and have a drink or two".

"Or five!" Aiden said with playful sarcasm.

Aiden and Zoe had an unusual relationship. She was a free spirit (read, wild child) and loved to antagonize Aiden, just for the fun of it. Aiden was a deep thinker and enjoyed verbally jousting with her, as she was a worthy opponent. Not that Amy wasn't bright herself, but Aiden so adored her, he didn't want to roast her in the way he did Zoe, not even as a joke. Actually, Zoe thought that the two of them together were just sickening sweet.

Zoe showed up at the apartment around 7 o'clock. When Amy opened the door, the two girls exchanged smiles and hugs, playfully kissing each other on either side of their cheeks, like they were greeting each other as they do in "the old country". They giggled as they walked down the hall to the living room where there was a bottle of wine and two glasses waiting.

"Hey, would you like some cheese?" Amy asked, as if she had just come up with a great idea.

"No, Aiden can just stay in his room and read his book," Zoe said with a little smirk.

"I heard that!" Aiden said loudly from the bedroom, feigning annoyance.

Aiden poked his head from around the corner and looked at Zoe, waiting for her to notice him. When he caught her eye, she glared at him and said, "*THERE* it is."

Without saying a word, he slowly slipped back out of

sight.

"No, come and join us" Zoe said.

Amy spoke like a begging child, "Yeah, spend time with us. You can read your book any time, but we only get to see Zoe once in a while."

Aiden peeked back out from behind the corner, rolling his eyes in disgust. He walked into the kitchen, took out a tumbler and made himself a whiskey on the rocks. Walking quickly back into the living room, he sat cross-legged on the couch next to Amy. Taking a big loud slurp of his whiskey, he smacked his lips and asked, "So, what are we going to talk about?"

Zoe started in on him right away, "I hear you have a new book about dreams, tell me all about it."

With a suddenly more serious tone, Aiden replied, "Well, I'm sure Amy's told you all about my bad dreams and lack of sleep. I thought I might do a little research to see if I could figure out something that will help me."

"You know what I think about dreams don't you?" Zoe asked.

Aiden closed his eyes, sucked his lips into his mouth, and slowly shook his head. Like she was setting up a volleyball to be spiked, Zoe proclaimed, "I think dreams are more real than the so-called real world."

Aiden retorted, "Is that where this conversation is going? I have real problems and you want to start off with something so ridiculous?"

"Oh no, here we go," said Amy, flopping back on the couch, taking a big sip of wine and looking at the two of them like she was ready to watch a fight.

Zoe launched into her diatribe. "It's not ridiculous. Tell me, when you think of yourself, who are you? Is your physical body you or is it your mind? Just because you can touch and feel your physical body doesn't mean that's who you are. Your mind, your intangible mind is who you are. Have you ever felt like a bug was crawling on your arm, only to look down and see nothing there? And when you go to the dentist and get a shot of Novocain, does the fact that you can't feel your cheek mean that your cheek isn't there? Physicality does not dictate reality. Just because you feel it, doesn't mean it's there. Just because you can't feel it, doesn't mean it's not. Let me explain it another way: Look at yourself in that mirror over there. The image is exactly like you, yet you're looking at the mirror and saying that's not real, that's not you. You are the physical reality and what is in the mirror is the dream. How do you know which is which?"

Amy spun around and looked directly at Aiden, eyebrows high and eyes wide open as if to say, *"...and your reply Sir?"* Aiden took a deep breath and let it out slowly. He began to speak with calming tone that would hopefully avoid any escalation in the fervor of the discussion.

"Okay, the bug and the Novocain, I'll give it to you. There can be a disconnect between perception and reality. I will also admit that the connection between the mind and the body is somewhat of a mystery, but you lost your footing with the mirror analogy. It would be very simple to tell what was real and what wasn't. If you threw a rock at me, I would feel the pain and probably scream 'Ouch!', and some other expletives. If you threw a rock at the mirror, the mirror would shatter and the image would be gone. No pain, no response, no reality. Why dreams are not the real reality is also easy to prove. In our waking lives, the real world, there is continuity and consequences. Every morning when I wake up, I pick up just where I left off when I went to bed the night before. If I injure myself on one day, the next day I still feel it. Even when I'm sleeping, the real world still carries on with its continuity and consequences. If I light a candle just before I go to bed, when I wake up, I can see that it has continued to burn throughout the night and gotten smaller. On the other hand, nothing that happens in the dream world has continuity nor consequence. In one dream, I'm a rock star on a stage in front of thousands of screaming fans, the next dream I'm back in high school and I have to take a test that I haven't studied for, and the next dream I'm running away from aliens in the woods. No continuity. In one dream I fall off a cliff and in another I'm crashing my car on a bridge, but when I wake up, I am unharmed. There are no consequences for any action I take in my dreams."

Amy spun back around towards Zoe with a look of pride on her face for her boyfriend's response. Zoe put her wine glass down on the coffee table, leaned in close towards Aiden with her elbows on her knees and stared intently into his eyes.

"If an artist paints a landscape, then paints a portrait, and then makes an abstract painting, is she not a real artist because she lacks continuity? If some sicko rapes a little girl and gets away with it, is there no crime because there was no consequence? The mind that gives you dreams when you sleep is the same mind that controls your body when you're awake. Action follows thought. First you think it, and then you do it. You think to yourself, *'I want to stand up.'* and then your body stands up. How is it that your intangible mind, those strange fluctuations in the ether, can control your physical body? In the waking world physicality restrains what your mind can do. In the dream world, your mind does whatever it wants. The dream world is your true self and therefore more real than the so-called real world."

With that, Aiden looked Zoe in the eyes and said aloud, "I want to stand up."

He stood up, walked back into the kitchen, and poured himself another whiskey. He sucked it down quickly, put the glass in the sink, and began walking toward the bedroom saying, "None of this is going to help me." He gently closed the door behind him.

"Aiden!" Zoe called out with an apologetic tone.

"I'll be right back," Amy said to Zoe as she got up to follow Aiden into the bedroom. She opened the bedroom door to find Aiden lying in bed reading his new book. She sat next to him on the bed and stroked his hair saying, "You know Zoe, she's always up for it. She doesn't mean anything by it, it's just her way of having fun."

Aiden rested the book on his chest and looked at Amy. "It's fine, I just don't have the energy for it right now. Go back and have fun with your friend and tell her I'm not mad."

"Okay sweetie," Amy said, giving him a kiss on the forehead, "I hope you have a good night".

2 Listen to Your Mother

Aiden didn't sleep much that night. Maybe he was still fired up about the discussion with Zoe or maybe it was too much whiskey, but either way he found plenty of time to read. Amy could sleep through anything, including Aiden's tossing and turning, or reading books, or turning on the television...anything. He was happy that his problem didn't become hers, but he would often feel envious as he looked at her resting peacefully. After a long day at work, with his head bobbing in front of a computer screen, Aiden called Amy to remind her he was going over to his best friend Brendan's house after work to eat dinner and just hang out for a while. Amy liked it when Aiden spent time with Brendan because Brendan was a good balance for him, plus, when Aiden was out of the apartment, Amy would use the free time to make her custom-crafted cat toys that she sold at the local pet store... Unique, high-end stuff that provided not only a creative outlet, but a little extra income too.

Aiden arrived at Brendan's house with a six pack of beer and some ribeyes for the grill. When he rang the bell, he heard a voice through the open windows.

"Out back, come on in!"

Aiden opened the door and walked through the small, well-kept house into the kitchen. Music was playing on the stereo, something Aiden had never heard before, but that wasn't unusual; Brendan always listened to bands that were somewhat off the beaten path. Aiden put the beers in the fridge, took a couple back out and opened the sliding screen door that led to the deck where Brendan was lighting the gas grill.

"Hey buddy" Aiden said as he handed Brendan a beer.

"Thank you, sir," Brendon replied with a smile and then reached for the bottle opener.

Clinking their bottles together, they looked each other in the eyes as they said, "Health and happiness!"

Brendan was a different kind of guy: he was smart, neat, and somewhat conservative...not in a political way, but more in a deliberately careful way of navigating through life. He was a few years older than Aiden, in his early 30s, but already had his own business, a house, a nice car, and savings and investments that would lead to a comfortable retirement. His attire was simple, his humor dry, his thinking logical and reasonable. He had a good dose of common sense and street-smarts that Aiden often likened to wisdom. Brendan was a big guy. He was tall and thick, but not fat. He kept his black hair cut short in a flat top and wore glasses with large black horn-rim frames, most likely to offset the size of his nose. Friends would tease him and say he looked like he had time traveled here from the 50s. Aiden never knew Brendan to have a girlfriend, as he was somewhat of a loner and "not so smooth with the ladies", but once anyone got to know him, he was great company and a really good friend to have.

Brendan threw the steaks on the grill, closed the lid, and started a timer. He took a sip of his beer and looked up at the sky as if he was searching for words. Turning to Aiden, he said, "You look tired my friend. Still having trouble sleeping?"

Aiden sighed, "It's brutal. It feels like every day I get just a little more beaten-down. I don't know how much lower I can go."

"And the bad dreams?"

Aiden rolled his eyes, "More now than ever."

With a sort of quiet confidence, and in a comforting tone, Brendan stated, "Well, I know all of the things that you've tried, maybe it's time to try something else."

There was nothing Aiden could have wanted more than to have some words of wisdom from Brendan that could help him with his insomnia. "Go on." Aiden said, trying to play down his hopeful interest.

Brendan continued, "I've been thinking about you lately, your bad dreams, and your problems sleeping, so

I decided to do some research on the Internet concerning alternative methods to combat nightmares and insomnia. What I found seems a little on the outside, but it can't hurt to try. Have you ever heard of binaural beats?"

"I've heard of them, but have no idea what they are. How can they help?"

Brendan explained, "Well, from what I gathered, our minds operate at different frequencies for different states of being. If you're relaxed, your brain is operating at one frequency and if you are stressing, at a different one. Binaural beats are putting a different tone, or frequency, into each ear via headphones, let's say like 100 Hz in one ear and 110 in the other. That means 10 times per second the wavelengths will interact in an audible way that is called beating. Because you're using headphones, the two tones are not actually interacting. Your brain is combining the two frequencies and producing the beat itself. It is believed that using two frequencies that produce a beat in the frequency range of brainwaves associated with relaxation or sleep will entrain, or encourage, your brain to align with that state of mind."

Aiden looked at Brendan, jokingly in disbelief, and said, "Whhaaatttt?!"

They both laughed. Brendan said, "I took the liberty of downloading some tone generating software and burning you a CD with the appropriate frequencies to produce the beats that you need. It's sitting on the kitchen table. It's the one with the picture of sheep jumping over a fence drawn on it."

Aiden could feel his eyes tearing up. He fought hard to not let it show, but could not resist walking over to Brendan and giving him a hug.

"Thanks so much man. I'm lucky to have you as a friend."

Brendan gave him a reassuring pat on the back and said, "Anytime buddy."

The rest of the night the two of them enjoyed a pleasurable evening together: drinking beer, eating dinner, listening to music, and just chatting about whatever came into their minds. Just the thought of a possible solution to his problem gave Aiden hope, a hope he had not had for quite some time.

On the way home from Brendan's house, Aiden decided to call his mom, whom he hadn't spoken to in a few weeks.

"Hey mom, how are you?" Aiden asked with an apologetic tone, knowing it had been too long since they last spoke.

"Well, well, well, to what do I owe the extreme honor of speaking to Sir Aiden?" his mother quipped.

"I know, I know, it's been a little while. I've been busy and haven't been sleeping well and things just seem to get away from me."

"Still not sleeping well sweetie? Still having the bridge dream?"

Aiden confided to his mom, "No, still not sleeping well. Yes, still having the bridge dream. I have been looking into it though and bought a book on dreams to try and figure out why I'm having this dream over and over. According to the book, the dream is reoccurring because whatever is causing it is still happening in my life. As far as it being the bridge dream, it said that this dream represents a fear of change. A bridge takes you safely from one place to another over some sort of hazard; a river, or a gorge, a railroad track, and the fact that I can't make it across the bridge tells me I'm afraid something bad is going to happen or I'm afraid of whatever the change is, or that I'll fail. I still haven't figured out why am having it, because everything seems to be going pretty well, but whatever it is, I hope to figure it out soon."

Now with a more analytical tone, Aiden's mom began to think aloud, "Hmmm, so you're afraid of something, but you don't know what it is. You've been having these dreams for about six months. Let's go back and try and figure out what happened about six months ago that you could be afraid of. You've been at the same job for about three years, so I don't think it's work. You've been living in the same town since you started college, so that can't be it. Wait a minute, you've been living with Amy for almost a year, how's everything going there?"

Aiden replied confidently, "Everything is going great. We get along really well. We spend a lot of time together, yet give each other enough room. She's supportive, kind, beautiful, I love her! I couldn't be happier with Amy."

"If I were to ask Amy how it was going, what do you think she would say?"

Once again, Aiden replied confidently, "I think she feels the same as I do. She's often told me how happy she is that we found each other and how good we are together. We have disagreements once in a while, but they are quickly settled with intelligent conversation and a little bit of compromise. The only thing I think she might complain about would be that she would like to get married, and me, not so much."

"Bingo! I'll bet you that's it!" exclaimed Aiden's mom.

"What's it?"

Aiden's mom started in on him, "You're afraid to get married. You're afraid of commitment, just like every other man. It makes perfect sense: the dreams started a few months after you moved in together. Everything else in your life is going well and has been pretty much unchanged. That bridge is taking you from the single life to married life and that scares you. If everything is going so well with you and Amy, and you've been living together for about a year now, what are you afraid of?"

"I'm not *AFRAID* of anything." Aiden said defensively, "I just have certain thoughts about marriage that Amy and I don't see eye to eye on. Listen, I'm almost home, I'm going go now, but I promise it won't be so long before my next call."

Aiden's mom prodded him a little more, "That's it, run away, run away! I got news for you, young man, if you want the dreams to stop, I'd say you either need to shit or get off the pot!"

"Ughh!"

"I love you!" Aiden's mom said in a sing-song way.

"I love you too mom," Aiden offered begrudgingly, "bye."

"Bye-bye sweetie."

Aiden pulled into the parking lot of the apartment complex, dragged himself out of the car and followed the meandering walk through the nicely landscaped grounds to the door of the apartment. As he was putting the key in the lock, his next-door neighbor's cat came out of the bushes, meowing loudly. Aiden knelt down and pet the cat as it rubbed its head on his feet, with its butt high up in the air. Talking in a high-pitched voice, something Aiden could not control when speaking to an animal, he said, "Hello Sweet Pea. How's the Whispering Pines welcoming committee tonight?"

The cat flopped over onto its side as Aiden rubbed behind its ears. He decided to sit down on the sidewalk next to the cat and pet it for a while.

"Oh yes, dat's the spot! Oh yes, my little baby loves dat."

Suddenly, Aiden got the sense that he was being

watched and looked up to see Amy staring at him through the window by the front door with a big smile on her face. She opened the door and sat down on the sidewalk with the cat in between them and said, "Let me get in on this cuddle session."

As they both were petting the cat, which was now laying on its back, legs spread wide, eyes closed, and purring loudly, Amy asked, "How was Brendan's tonight?"

Still speaking in his high-pitched cat voice, Aiden squeaked, "Oh it was very good, yes it was. It's always good at Brendan's house. He's my bestest buddy."

"Are you talking to me now or the cat?" Amy asked playfully.

They both got up, said their goodbyes to Sweet Pea and walked inside. Aiden took Amy in his arms, kissed her gently on the lips and gave her a nice long hug. He spoke softly, "Look, I'm really tired, big surprise, so I'm going to turn in early. We can talk about things over dinner tomorrow night. Okay?"

"That's fine, I have a little more work to do on my cat toys. Sleep well sweetie."

Amy gave him another kiss, then Aiden turned and slowly walked into the bedroom. Aiden slept that night, but he had the dream again.

3 We Need to Talk

The next day at work went pretty well for Aiden. He was working in the field and that was always better when he was feeling tired. Walking around in the sunshine and fresh air helped keep him awake and alert, unlike sitting in front of a computer screen all day. Also, he felt a much more direct connection to nature, and an increased sense of protecting it, when he was actually, physically, working in it. He couldn't wait to get home and talk to Amy about what Brendan had done for him. He had already decided that he would try using the binaural beats for the first time that night. However, at the same time, gnawing away at him, was the conversation that he had with his mom. He didn't know if she was right or not, but he realized the more he thought about it the more uncomfortable he became. If that was it, what would he do about it? He didn't want to get married, but he would never want to leave Amy. He had always felt a little guilty, knowing she wanted to get married and that it was he who was keeping it from happening. The thing about physical labor is that it leaves your mind free to think about whatever it wants. All day long, Aiden went back and forth between hopeful thoughts for sleep that night and dreading a conversation he knew he would have to have with Amy.

On the way home from work that night, Aiden picked up some Chinese food for Amy and him to have for dinner. When he got home, he walked inside, put the food down on the table and said, "Hey darling, just let me take a quick shower and then we can eat."

"Okay, I'll set the table." Amy said without looking up, as she pulled the dead leaves off of the plant by the window.

Not planning to go anywhere after dinner, Aiden came out in his PJs.

"I see you dressed for the occasion." Amy said with a smirk.

"Hey if it was good enough for Hef..."

With one eyebrow raised, head tilted to the side, hands on her hips, Amy retorted, "I sincerely doubt that Hef walked around in an old T-shirt and a pair of boxer shorts!" Amy quickly changed her expression to that of a polite schoolgirl asking a question in class, "So, what's for dinner?"

"Moo Shu pork, pan seared green beans, and vegetable stuffed dumplings. Yum, Yum!"

"Ooh, I love it!"

"I know, that's why I got it." Aiden said with a loving smile.

The two sat down to eat their meal, sharing their stories from the day's work: Amy had trouble catching a fisher cat for its monthly weigh-in and Aiden saw a hellbender as he worked on repairing a footbridge that crossed a stream on the Blue Falls Loop Trail. Then Aiden told Amy about what Brendan had done for him. He explained, as best as he could, about the binaural beats and told Amy he was hopeful about trying it out that evening. It was a nice relaxing evening for the two of them. After dinner, Aiden loaded the dishwasher while Amy cleaned the table. When they were through, they went into the living room and sat on the couch together. Aiden could feel his stress level rising as he thought about the conversation he had with his mom and how Amy might react to it.

"So, I talked to my mom yesterday and we had an interesting conversation." Aiden said tentatively.

"Oh really, what about?"

Aiden took a deep breath and thought about how he would put it. He looked at Amy sitting on the couch, legs crossed, facing him, with her beautiful green eyes looking at him, waiting to hear what he would say. She could sense his apprehension and so she reached out and put her hand on his knee and gave him a supportive look that said, *"Go ahead."* Just then, the doorbell rang. *"Saved by the bell,"* Aiden thought to himself.

"Hold that thought, I'll get the door" Amy offered.

"Make sure you look through the peephole first."

Amy put her eye to the peephole and exclaimed, "It's Zoe!"

"For the first time, I'm actually glad she's here," Aiden said under his breath.

The two ladies walked into the living room. Amy took her spot on the couch next to Aiden and Zoe in the chair across from them.

"Back so soon? I thought we would get at least a few days off." Aiden poked.

Zoe spoke in a tone that was uncharacteristically repentant. "Well, I was thinking about the other night and wanted to come by and apologize. I know that not being able to sleep is a serious thing and I didn't mean to rattle your cage... that much. Also, I got you a little something."

"And what would that be."

"Not now, later. Just you and me."

"Hmmm" Amy vocalized, feigning mistrust.

Aiden looked at the two of them. When they were together, the energy in the room was different: playful and upbeat. He began to think it might work in his favor talking to Amy with Zoe there, her presence taking the edge off the conversation, so he started, "As I was saying, I was talking to my mom yesterday about the book I have been reading about dreams. I told her about the interpretation of the bridge dream and she had an interesting take on it."

"The bridge dream," Zoe offered, "about being afraid of a transition in your life?"

Surprised, Aiden looked at her, "Yes, exactly. How would *YOU* know?"

"After the other night, I was feeling bad about things, so I thought I might look into it a bit...see if I could help."

Aiden continued, "She seems to think it's because I'm afraid to get married."

Amy looked at Aiden. The look in her eyes was both hope and sadness at the same time. Aiden can tell she didn't know which way the conversation was going to go. Zoe noticed it as well and said, "Okay, take it easy sister. Let the man speak."

Aiden began to speak, with a calm, quiet, confidence, "All right, since Zoe is here, let me give a little background information: I personally do not believe in marriage. It always seems to be tied up in religion, which I am also not a fan of. Furthermore, it is completely unfair to a man's biological programming, that has been engrained in him for hundreds of thousands of years. You see, males and females in the animal world have different ways of ensuring that their genes are passed on, which is the goal of all living things. In nature, the male tries to impregnate as many females as possible in order to achieve the goal. The female protects and raises her offspring in order to achieve that same goal. Which method do you think marriage favors? Obviously, the female's. In marriage, the female gets exactly the scenario in which she has been programmed to operate. The male gets the exact opposite of his programming. It's unfair. When you think about it logically, there is no other situation in life that one handles the way one handles marriage. As an adult, do we pick one outfit and wear that one outfit every single day for the rest of our lives? Do we pick one favorite food and eat only that food every meal for the rest of our lives? Do we pick one job and do only that one job, for that one company, for the rest of our lives? The obvious answer to all of those questions is an emphatic no! Why then should we do that with our relationships. Pick one and that's it for the rest of your life. It doesn't make any sense. There are hapless romantics and religious buffoons who claim that out of a world of over 7 billion people, there is only one person that you could marry; one true love in the entire world. Isn't it funny, that their perfect match always happens to live in the same place they do? It's never that someone's perfect match lives on the other side of the world and they never meet. No, they are always right there. And to all the people who get divorced or widowed and then get married again, what do they have to say about that. Amy, I love you more than my own life, but if I was born in New York City, or Austin Texas, or Budapest Hungary, or bumfuck Egypt, I would be having this conversation with someone else right now. I believe a person could marry one of hundreds, maybe even thousands of people and be just as happy. Why would you want to limit your relationships? Why would you want to limit love?"

"Limit love? Don't you mean limit sex?" Zoe said.

"Absolutely not! When I say love, I mean love. When I mean sex, I will say sex."

"Well, aren't love and sex pretty much the same thing? Isn't sex the physical representation of love?" asked Amy.

"Now this is a whole different problem. Love and sex have nothing to do with each other."

"What?!"

"We are lied to about both of them from childhood. People are so ashamed of what they do with their own bodies that they can't even talk about it directly. They call it 'sleeping together' or 'having carnal knowledge' or the worst of all, 'making love'. No one can call sex what it is: sex. Some guy is singing a love song and he says, 'I want to make love to you all night long'. What he's really saying is, 'I want to have sex with you all night long'. You can't make love. You either feel love for someone, or you don't. There is no 'making it.' Not to mention, I don't know one guy who could actually have sex all night long. The idea doesn't even sound good, imagine the chafing!"

Everyone laughed. Aiden would often intersperse his serious dialogue with humor in order to keep his audience at ease. He could also tell you things he knows you don't want to hear with a smile on his face and a playful tone that somehow helped mitigate the negative reaction of the listener. Aiden continued, "The whole love song genre is based on stringing together a bunch of ridiculous lies. 'I would swim across the ocean for you, I would jump over the moon for you, I would die 1000 deaths to spend one minute with you'… Bullshit! And every time you see a scene in the movies, or on TV, where a parent is about to have 'the talk' with one of their children, it always starts off with, 'When a man and a woman love each other very much….' Tell me, is every time you've had sex because you and someone else were so deeply in love?

Aiden looked at Amy. She looked down and shook her head no. Aiden turned to Zoe. With a devilish grin on her face, she stared Aiden in the eyes and slowly shook her head, no.

"I love my mom. I do not want to have sex with her! I love my sister. I do not want to have sex with her! I love the old woman who lived next door to me when I was growing up. She would babysit me when I was a little boy. She is the sweetest, kindest, most loving woman you could ever meet. I do not want to have sex with her! On the other hand, there is a woman at work, Ashley, who I cannot stand. Her personality, her mannerisms, her beliefs… make me sick, but she is *SO* hot, I want to fuck her brains out! Sex has nothing to do with love."

"Well, I guess that depends on how you define love. The love you have for your mother, your sister, or your babysitter, is different than the love you have for your significant other." Amy calmly stated.

"I disagree. I think love is one thing: when you care

about someone else more than yourself; when someone else's happiness is more important than your own. When you would rather suffer than have someone you care about suffer, that is love. Based on that definition, you can see how it is possible to love more than one person. Just because you are sexually attracted to someone you love, doesn't make that a different kind of love. It's just love and sex at the same time. Two great things that go great together!"

Everyone laughed again.

Amy looked at Aiden like a little girl trying to convince her parents to let her have a kitten and said, "Well, if all that is true, then you would marry me because you love me and that's what would make me happy."

"Checkmate!" Zoe exclaimed, her eyes locked on to Aiden's and waited for a response.

"Okay, let's pause right there and perhaps we can continue this conversation in private." Aiden said as he slowly turned towards Zoe. "I believe you had something for me before you go?"

"Okay, I can take a hint, especially when you bash me over the head with it. Aiden, why don't you walk me out to my car."

Zoe collected her things and started for the door.

"I'll be right back sweetheart." Aiden said to Amy as he stood up to follow Zoe out.

The two walked out to the car without saying a word. Zoe unlocked the car, through her things on the passenger seat and reached into the center console. She pulled something out and wrapped her hand tightly around it. She extended her arm, palm down and waited for Aiden to hold out his hand. Aiden reached out to receive whatever it was she was concealing. A small orange bottle with a white cap dropped into his hand. The bottle was filled with peach colored, oval shaped pills.

"Xanax. Take one of these at bedtime and I guarantee, you will sleep!"

Looking puzzled Aiden asked, "Don't you need a prescription for this? Aren't these a controlled substance? How did you get these?"

"Yes, yes, and none of your business. If you need more, just ask...and try not to get hooked on them. I understand they are quite addictive."

Zoe leaned in and gave Aiden a kiss on the cheek. "Okay, now I'm paid up."

"I'm not sure this is for me, but, thank you, seriously."

Zoe smiled, sat down in the car, and closed the door. Aiden took a step back still looking at her somewhat in disbelief as she started the engine, looked over her shoulder and backed out of the parking spot. She gave a wink and a wave, then chirped the tires as she sped away. Aiden put the bottle in his pocket and began to walk back to the apartment. Although taking prescription medicine was not something he preferred to do, the thought of actually having control over whether or not he was going to sleep that night did seem very appealing. He weighed the pros and cons in his head hoping for a clear winner. As he got closer to the apartment, his thoughts turned to continuing the conversation with Amy alone. Approaching the front door, he saw Sweet Pea sitting on the welcome mat, back leg pointing straight up into the air, licking his nether regions. Aiden stooped down and gave him a few pets and said in his high, squeaky voice, "It's my choice if I sleep tonight. Yes, it is!"

Back inside the apartment, Aiden told Amy about the gift Zoe had given him.

"That girl, I swear," Amy said, smiling and shaking her head.

"Yeah, she's a peach of a gal. Going to make some guy a happy man someday." In a suddenly more serious tone Aiden took Amy's hand, and spoke softly, "How about this, since we're both young and there are no children on the horizon, we hold off for a little while longer, give us both some more time to think. Maybe we can come up with an arrangement that we can both be happy with. Also, it's not impossible that I change my mind about this either, because I do want to make you happy. I promise not to keep you waiting for too long."

"Okay, fair enough. You know, I don't mean to pressure you and I respect your right to have your own opinion. I just don't want to feel like I'm wasting my life waiting for something that will never happen. I just need to have a little bit of hope."

"It's true I'm not sure about marriage, but there is no doubt in my mind, I'm sure about you."

The two of them embraced and kissed. Both of them felt a little bit of relief, release, and reassurance that everything was going to work out all right. Soon, the long, wet kisses began stoking the fires of passion they had for each other. Aiden slid off the couch, got down on one knee and worked his hands underneath Amy's shoulders and thighs. He scooped her up into his arms and stood up without ever leaving her lips. He carried her into their bedroom. They slowly undressed each other. Her warm breath blew in his ear. His soft lips kissed her neck. When they were both fully nude, he laid her down and straddled her. Gently touching her temples with his fingertips, he moved his hands downward in a swirling motion, ever so lightly touching her skin. He touched her face, her neck, her shoulders, her breasts, his fingertips circling gently around her body. When he reached her belly, all 10 fingers slid up and down, up and down her belly and the sides of her body, giving her goosebumps from head to toe. He moved backwards, slipping smoothly between her legs, his fingers now skimming across the sides of her butt, then around to the front, tickling her lower belly and inside her thighs, touching her everywhere, all around, except for the one place she yearned to be touched. Then a soft, gentle, kiss on her clit had her hips rolling forward as she moaned in ecstasy. A few more tender touches of his tongue on her sweet spot and then a long, slow lick, starting at the bottom of her flower and sliding all the way to the top. Again, and again, and again. Each pass pressing deeper than the last.

Amy spread her legs wide, her feet falling off each side of the bed, and lifted her butt off of the sheets, pressing her crotch into Aiden's face. Tightly gripping the headboard with her hands, her whole body shook uncontrollably as she came, "Oh my god. Fuck me. Fuck me!"

The two of them came together with a perfect synergy of lust and love, growing from all that was so good and so right with the two of them. It was one of the best times they had ever spent together. Amy came twice more and when Aiden had finished, they laid there together in each other's arms, full of content and absorbed with love.

A short while later, Aiden noticed that Amy had fallen asleep. He gently slipped his arm out from beneath her and laid her head on her pillow. He rolled out of the bed and pulled the covers up to her neck. After using the bathroom and brushing his teeth he went into the living room and found the CD that Brendan had made for him. Unplugging the headphones from the computer he grabbed an old Walkman out of a box in the closet and headed for the bedroom. He quietly got into bed, making sure not to wake Amy. It felt a little strange preparing to do what he was about to do, but he wanted to do it all the same. Aiden put in the CD, put on the headphones and hit play. He adjusted the volume so he could hear the tones clearly beating, but not so loud that it would keep him up. Lifting the earpiece off of one year and then the other, he could hear each side was playing one clear tone, but when he had both earpieces on, he heard the beating in his mind even though he knew it wasn't really there. The fact that it was doing what Brendan said it would, gave him even more hope that it might actually work. Being a big fan of the shotgun approach, Aiden decided to begin concentrating on his breathing as well. In through the nose, out through the mouth, in through the nose, out through the mouth. His breathing was slow, steady, and measured. He then directed his thoughts to relaxing his body, thinking of each part and then focusing on having it release the tension it was holding. As his body let go, he felt himself sinking more deeply into the bed. Trying to forget about the worries of the world, and the burdens that he bared, he concentrated on everything good in his life and all that he loved about it. Looking at the moonlit shadows of the trees dancing on the wall in front of him, Aiden's eyes grew heavy. A short while after he had begun, Aiden was asleep.

4 Troubling News

"Not bad for a first try," Aiden thought to himself, as he lay awake in bed the next morning. Although months of not sleeping well can't be corrected in one night, he did feel noticeably better having slept more than usual. *"A decent night's sleep preceded by one of the best times Amy and I have ever had together... I could get used to this."* Aiden thought about his buddy Brendan, which brought a smile to his face, "Brendan is the fucking man!" he said aloud. As Aiden began to get ready for work, he thought how much he would like to tell Brendan about his success and thank him again for his help. Amy was going to run errands on her way home from work that night, so Aiden thought it would be the perfect opportunity to swing by Brendan's. He texted Brendan, knowing that he would be awake already, being the early riser that he was.

Brendan quickly responded with a counter offer, *"How about drinks and appetizers at the Ginger House?*

My treat. Landed a new account and feel like celebrating!"

"Perfect, I feel like celebrating too!" Aiden replied.

Aiden was enjoying another day in the field, continuing his work on the footbridge. When the crew broke for lunch, he grabbed his backpack and hiked off to a secluded spot, about 10 minutes away. There was a rock outcropping there that he liked to visit. He leaned up against a large rock that jutted up out of the ground on the side of a hill. It overlooked the stream with a nice view of the cove where the flow from numerous spring heads converged to create it. On the menu today: A Havarti cheese sandwich with sprouts, baby spinach, and spicy Chinese mustard, a bag of smoked almonds, and some dried dates for dessert ("Hippie food" as Zoe would call it). He took out his book on dreams and began thumbing through it to see if there was anything else of interest to read while he was on break. Aiden noticed there was an appendix entitled *Lucid Dreaming.* The writer explained that lucid dreaming was dreaming while being aware of the fact that you are dreaming. Often times, someone who is lucid dreaming can control what happens in their dream. If one dreams that they are running away from some sort of danger, yet it feels like they are running with their legs knee-deep in molasses, a lucid dreamer might be able to decide to fly instead. If one dreams they are back in high school and walking through the halls without any clothes on, a lucid dreamer may be able to duck into a locker room and find clothes to wear in an open locker. Aiden thought to himself, *"If one were to dream about driving a car up a dangerously steep bridge, perhaps a lucid dreamer would be able to stop, or turn around, or take a ferry to get across."* The writer went on to explain different actions one could take in order to encourage oneself to lucid dream: Asking oneself throughout the waking day "Am I dreaming right now?" may encourage one to ask the same question while dreaming. Upon waking from a dream, repeating to oneself continuously, "I will be aware while I dream," as one waits to fall back asleep may give one the awareness they desire. There were also signs to look for while dreaming to alert the dreamer to the fact that they are dreaming: Looking at a clock to check the time, then, look away and then back again to see if the time is still the same. In a dream, it will often be different every time you look. Try pressing one's finger through the palm of the opposite hand. Impossible in the real world, but commonly done in a dream state. The one that really grabbed Aiden's attention was being aware of common themes in one's dreams. If one often dreams of being lost in a maze, remind oneself of that often during the waking day. When it occurs in a dream, one may be able to recognize that theme as a sign they are dreaming. It even mentioned the use of binaural beats as a way to encourage lucid dreaming. *"If I can continue to have success sleeping with the binaural beats, being able to control my bad dreams would make it even better."* Aiden read on with increasing interest. Had he not set a timer on his cell phone, he would have been late back from lunch for sure.

After work, Aiden went home, took a quick shower, and headed back out to the Ginger House. As usual, it was almost impossible to find a parking spot downtown. The quirky, artsy, downtown area was small, but very popular. There really wasn't ever a "season" there, but a constant mass of tourists and local pleasure seekers packing the sidewalks, shops, and restaurants. Street performers were on almost every corner. Psychics offered to tell your fortune, artists drew caricatures, and musicians played original songs, all for a small donation dropped into a box, a hat, or an open instrument case. Circling the block like a vulture over a dead possum, Aiden spied a space opening up on the other side of the street. A quick scan for cops, then Aiden pulled a U-ie and grabbed the spot. Jumping out of his car, Aiden started down the crowded sidewalk towards the Ginger House. Just as he was about to enter, he saw Brendan coming from the other way and waved his hand over his head to get his attention. The two walked in together and sat down at the bar. Brendan ordered a gin and tonic with a twist of lime and Aiden his Ginger House go-to drink: whiskey in a sweet and spicy ginger beer. Pot stickers, crab Rangoon, and shrimp tempura rolls rounded out the order. When they got their drinks, they clinked their glasses together, looked each other in the eye and said, "Health and Happiness".

"Congratulations on the new account. Glad to hear business is booming!"

"Thank you, sir. I'm in a good place. Word is getting around and new clients are coming to me! What are you celebrating?"

"I tried the binaural beats for the first time last night and I slept better than usual."

"That's great news! I'm so happy for you"

"All thanks to you my good friend."

"So, what else is going on, anything?"

"Well, Zoe gave me some prescription drugs to help me sleep, which is pretty much illegal."

"Amy's friend, right? What is she like? I mean, besides being a drug dealer."

"Zoe is wild! A free spirit, a thrill seeker, and one of the most uninhibited people I've ever met. She's smart, smoking hot, and totally aggravating. Constantly up in my shit and just loves to push my buttons. They say opposites attract, and I think that's why she is Amy's best friend. Amy is kind and mellow and demure and Zoe is the opposite of that."

"Tell me more about this, 'smoking hot'."

"She's about 5'8, 135 pounds; long, straight, thick, shiny, black hair to the middle of her back; light brown skin; those almond-shaped, cat eyes; a fine, slightly up-turned nose; big, wide, Julia Roberts smile with perfect white teeth; C cups that she wears up high; slender, yet curvy body; tight, round ass; long, athletic, shapely legs... She's so hot, it's ridiculous."

"Sounds interesting. She seeing anyone?"

"Dude, she would eat you alive! Trust me, you don't want any part of that."

"Not even a little part?"

"No!"

"How 'bout you? If you were a free agent, would you go for it?"

"Relationship wise, hell no! But on a physical level, fuck yeah!"

"You're a pig."

The two finished their food and drinks, then walked around downtown for a bit, just to see the sights and feel the energy of the crowd. Throughout the night, Aiden repeated to himself, "Am I dreaming right now?" Brendan heard him and gave a curious look. When Aiden explained what he was doing, Brendan poked, "One night of good sleep and now you want to control your dreams!"

A few bottled waters later, they decided to call it a night. Aiden shook Brendan's hand and thanked him for his generosity. A hug with a few pats on the back, and they parted company.

Aiden got back to the apartment about 9 o'clock, a little later than he was shooting for. When he walked through the door, he looked up to see Amy standing at the end of the hall, looking very upset. Aiden thought it was because he was out later than expected and forgot to call and let Amy know.

"Oh sweetie, I'm sorry I didn't call and let you know that I was going to be late. Do you forgive me?"

"Yes, I forgive you, but that's not why I'm upset."

Aiden followed Amy into the living room. He could hear that someone was in the bathroom and gave Amy a look like, *"Who's that?"* Just then, the bathroom door open and Zoe stepped out. She looked different, not in her appearance as much as her demeanor. Gone were the bright eyes and wicked smile she normally greeted Aiden with, instead, she winced a little bit as she said, "Hey Aiden."

The two girls sat down and Amy motioned for Aiden to take a seat. It wasn't the usual lighthearted energy in the room, but one of tension. No one was saying a word. Aiden sat there, looking back and forth between the two of them, waiting for someone to say something. Amy spoke up.

"Zoe, why don't you tell Aiden why I am upset."

"Well, Amy is upset with me because of my new job. You know how I bounce around from place to place and just can't seem to hold a job for very long. That means I'm never anywhere long enough to get a raise or a promotion. Things are just getting more and more expensive, yet I still seem to be making the same amount of money. So, I met this girl at the gym who seems very nice. We get along great together. A few nights ago, we went out to dinner and then went shopping. I noticed that she drives a nice car, wears the coolest clothes, expensive perfume, and buys whatever she wants. She's about the same age as me and I was wondering how she can afford all of that. So, I asked. Long story short, she got me a job where she works...at an escort service."

Amy turned and looked at Aiden, waiting for him to say something...anything to change Zoe's mind.

Aiden looked at Zoe tentatively and asked, "So, this escort service, it's like you go with some lonely, old, rich guy to a banquet as his date, or, you meet a sleazy loser in a hotel room to fuck?"

"Neither, well, kind of both. It's like I meet some lonely, old, rich guy at his house...and we fuck. My friend says our services are a lot more expensive than some streetwalking, hooker type. That weeds out the sleazy losers, you know, the riffraff. It's always at some really nice house or a luxury hotel room. The owner-"

"You mean pimp?" Amy snapped.

Zoe gave Amy a look, took a deep breath, turned to Aiden and continued. "The owner sets up all the work. He only accepts credit cards so he knows who we are dealing with. The charge shows up as Carmen Enterprises, so it's discrete for the customers. The girls rate all of their experiences and anyone who doesn't treat them right, will no longer get service. The clients are told this and it really keeps them in line. They all have to wrap it up and we get tested once a month. It's quite professional."

"I'm sure it is, the oldest ever!" Amy jabbed.

"How can it be worth it? I mean really. What's your pride worth?" Aiden asked.

"Pride? This may bother you, but it doesn't bother me. Not everyone can do this, they don't have the guts. And how good does it make me feel knowing that guys are willing to pay to be with me. This is new, different, and puts me a little bit outside of my comfort zone, which is where I like it. I think it's exciting and not only that, but in a few hours, I can make what it takes me all week to make at my regular job. I get 250 bucks a pop!"

"You might want to use a different term. I don't think anybody is popping anything on you!" Aiden said with a smirk.

"This is not a joke Aiden!" Amy barked, wiping the smirk from Aiden's face.

"I look at it this way: I get the money I want. The client gets what he wants. No one gets hurt. Everyone is happy. This isn't a life sentence. I'll only do it as long as I need to. Pay my credit cards off, get some new tires on the car, put some money into savings, maybe have enough to take some classes so I can get a real job, a career. Besides, I don't think it's a secret, I like fucking. I can close my eyes and think about Chris Hemsworth, Jason Momoa, or, even you Aiden," Zoe gave her trademark wink and devilish grin.

"... Aaaand she's back!" Aiden said.

"Oh my God Zoe, are you trying to make it worse?"

"Look, I promise I will be as careful as I can, always on my guard. I'll leave at the first hint of trouble. The owner will always know where I am and who I'm with. And if it makes you feel better, we just won't talk about it anymore."

"The only thing that will make me feel better is knowing you're not doing it. I'm not judging you. I'm worried about you. And I want you to know, that I still love you and always will."

Amy stood up, stepped towards Zoe, and held her arms out, signaling for a hug. Zoe rose up into her arms and the two embraced. Not the "leaning in, only shoulders touching" type of hug, but a full body hug, heads resting together, slowly rocking side to side. Both let tears roll down their cheeks. Zoe kissed Amy and said, "I love you too. You are such a good friend."

Zoe collected her things, said her goodbyes and left. Amy and Aiden didn't see her quite as often after that, but she made sure to send a text every now and then to let Amy know she was all right. They both thought about Zoe often, but in different ways. Amy was anxious for her friend and Aiden couldn't stop thinking to himself as he laid in bed at night, *"I wonder what Zoe is doing right now?"* On one hand, he felt bad for her, and on the other, he was almost proud of her. No matter what she said, he knew she had to feel some shame, but her guts and self-confidence were almost inspirational.

Over the next several weeks, Aiden was able to get more and more sleep with the binaural beats. It wasn't like everything was fixed instantly, but there was slow and steady improvement as time went on. He also employed many of the techniques used to encourage lucid dreaming, his favorite being, asking himself throughout the day, "Am I dreaming?" Amy found it a little bit strange, but tolerable. He did it so often, it got to the point he didn't realize he was doing it. Essentially, that was the point. If he did it enough while he was awake, it would become a habit and hopefully, one that would carry over into his dreams. If he did it while dreaming, it may be enough for him to realize his situation and begin having a little control over his dreams.

One day, the couple was downtown having lunch at a restaurant that had sidewalk dining. With people sitting all around, and passing by on the sidewalk, he casually said in between bites, "Am I dreaming?" Amy reached out and pinched him on the arm, which made him yelp like a puppy who got his paw stepped on. A woman who was just passing by at that moment was startled by the sound. She jumped back, her hands flew up and she let out a scream. Everyone sitting at the restaurant laughed, including many of the passersby.

"I guess not!" Amy quipped.

A few days later, Amy, Aiden, and Zoe were taking a hike together. It had been a long time since the two of them saw Zoe. Aiden walked behind while the two girls held hands and walked in front of him. It was a hot summer day and the three were heading to Aiden's favorite waterfall for a picnic lunch. The air was damp from the previous night's rain. The sweet smell of wildflowers hung thick in the air. Shining shafts of sunlight wove their way through the trees and made the stream sparkle with dancing light. Amy and Aiden were dressed in shorts and T-shirts with hiking sandals, but Zoe was wearing shiny, gold, skin-tight shorts with a black tube top and black pumps. She had gold chains draped around her neck and gold bracelets clanging on her wrists. Aiden thought her attire was odd and also found Amy's complete disregard of it unusual. Then Aiden said, "Am I dreaming?" The two girls ignored him as if they couldn't even hear him. He began to look around to see if anything else was unusual. Other than Zoe's attire everything seemed normal until he looked at the stream. They had been following the trail uphill to the waterfall for about half an hour but Aiden only now noticed the stream was flowing the same way. Finally, it happened! Aiden realized he was dreaming and decided to put it to the test. He told Amy he forgot something in the car and asked her to go back and get it. She gladly agreed and told the two to wait for her there until she came back. As soon as Amy was out of sight Aiden turned to Zoe and said,

"I can't believe how hot it is. How can you stand walking around in all those clothes? I think you'd be much more comfortable if you took them off."

Zoe looked at Aiden and said, "Good idea!"

She crossed her arms in front of herself, grabbed the bottom of her tube top, then pulled it up over her head. Holding it between her thumb and forefinger at arm's length, she dramatically opened her hand and let it drop to the ground. Zoe put her hand on Aiden's shoulder to steady herself as she balanced on one foot and then the other, sliding her shorts off. She turned to Aiden, struck a pose, and said, "Ta Da!"

Aiden could not believe his eyes. She was so beautiful. He felt a lump in his throat and one growing in his shorts. She walked up to him, standing just inches away and said, "What should we do now?"

Aiden pulled her into his arms. He could feel her hard nipples on his chest. Zoe stepped back and grabbed Aiden's hands, then once again pressed her body up against him and placed his hands on her ass. She stared into Aiden's eyes while her fingers ran through his long, thick, curly, hair. Pulling his head towards hers, she kissed him on the lips. Their mouths opened and...

Aiden woke to find himself lying in bed next to Amy. His heart was pounding, his head still reeling from the dream. He couldn't believe how real it felt, her hot tongue sliding in and out of his mouth. He lay in bed, thinking of those last few moments of the dream over and over again, hoping to fall asleep and pick up where he left off. Minute after minute, hour after hour he lay awake until he saw the light of dawn peeking in through the blinds and filling the room with an orange glow. *"Dammit! Of course, I can't fall back asleep after that."* As he lay in the quiet of the room, he could hear Amy breathing next to him. He felt a little guilty about what he chose to do in the dream, but then comforted himself thinking, *"No harm, no foul. It's just a dream. I didn't actually DO anything."*

.

5 EMOTIONAL OVERLOAD

As time went on, Amy noticed a change in Aiden, and like most things, there was a good side to it and a bad side to it. The fact that he was getting more sleep was great. He had more energy and a more positive attitude. Now that he wasn't tired all the time, they were able to spend more time together doing all the things that they loved to do: Hiking, camping, riding bikes, going downtown for a night out, catching a movie, trying to cook new things at home, going to concerts and of course, sex; Lots and lots of sex! On the down side, Aiden seemed somewhat consumed by his lucid dreaming. Sometimes he would sleep on the couch in the living room instead of sleeping with Amy in bed because he felt it was easier to focus on his meditation while listening to the binaural beats. On the weekends, he would often take naps in hopes of getting control of another dream. He even began taking the Xanax that Zoe gave him from time to time so that he could fall asleep faster and stay asleep longer. He had mentioned that he had trouble staying asleep once he realized that he was dreaming and hoped the Xanax would keep him from waking just when things were getting good.

Amy asked him, "And just what are you doing during these lucid dreams?"

Aiden replied with a big smile and his eyebrows jumping," Whatever I want!"

Amy felt bad that she was jealous of whatever it was Aiden was dreaming about and tried not to think about it too much. *"Anyway, I'm the one he's with in the real world."*

One Friday night, after a long week of work, Amy and Aiden decided to treat themselves and go out for dinner. As they were heading downtown, Aiden saw the parking lot by the greenway was almost empty. Making a split-second decision, he quickly pulled in.

"What are you doing?"

"I figured it's only about a mile from here to the restaurant, it's a beautiful night, and I don't want to ruin it getting frustrated looking for parking. Let's just walk from here."

"That's a great idea!"

The two got out of the car and began walking, hand-in-hand, down the winding greenway. Outside of downtown proper, the greenway was surrounded with lush grassy fields, a canopy of trees, rock outcroppings, and a nice little stream that weaved its way from side to side under the many footbridges. There were outdoor chess/checker tables, exercise stations, playground equipment, and little side trails that terminated with park benches that faced the stream. An old couple sat on one of the benches located just before reaching downtown.

It brought a smile to Amy's face and she said out loud, "Maybe one day that will be us."

"Maybe that is us and we've learned how to time travel and we're checking up on ourselves!"

Amy just smiled and shook her head knowing that Aiden was not really the romantic type. At least not in that way. Once they reached the area where downtown began, the stream disappeared into a culvert that channeled it beneath the city. Aiden always looked at it as the end of nature and the beginning of the concrete jungle. *"Both have their place, but if I had to choose one or the other, it would be nature."* When they were almost at the restaurant, Amy's phone rang.

"Zoe, it's so good to hear from you!... Well, we're not home right now. We just got downtown and are going out to dinner... How about tomorrow?... Our place, we'll cook for you... Say, 6 o'clock?... Perfect, we'll see you then."

"Don't hang up. I want to talk to her." Aiden whispered in Amy's year.

Amy gave Aiden a look of disbelief and said, "Hold on,

someone wants to talk to you."

"Hey Zoe, it's Aiden. How are you?... Doing good thanks... That's been going pretty good as well and kind of what I wanted to talk to you about. Would it be too much to ask you for another bottle of, well, you know? ... That would be great! Is there something I can do for you?... Aiden rolled his eyes, "No, I mean really. Is there anything I can do for you?... Okay, okay, thank you. I really appreciate it... I'll see you tomorrow, bye."

After dinner, as the couple made their way back to the car, Aiden's phone rang. Brendan was calling to ask a favor. He wanted to build a roof over one side of the deck so he could still use the grill and eat outside when it was raining. He already had all the lumber and other materials, but just needed a little extra muscle and know how to get the job done. Of course, Aiden was happy to help his friend. It was rare that he felt he could do anything for Brendan, so he jumped at the chance. Aiden had helped him build the deck a few years ago, so he was very familiar with what he was going to be working with. Going down a mental checklist of all the things that they would need for the project, Aiden rattled off an impressive collection of tools and materials. Brendan had them all. They planned on it taking the better part of the day to frame it up and another day, the next weekend, to put up the plywood and shingle the roof. Amy reminded Aiden to make sure he was back in time for dinner with Zoe.

"I'll make sure I'm back in time to get cleaned up before she gets there."

The next morning, Aiden arrived at Brendan's house ready to work. They planned, measured, and began cutting the wood and laying it out. As they worked, they listened to one of Brendan's esoteric, indie rock, playlists and talked about everything from politics to work to music to girls. No matter where they started, it always seemed to end up on girls. Around 10:30, Aiden walked over to the cooler and pulled out a beer.

"A little early for that don't you think?" Brendan asked.

"Am I sweating?"

"Yes."

"Time for beer!"

"Good point. Toss me one."

While they were taking a breather and having a drink, Aiden told Brendan about Zoe's new line of work, how Amy felt about it, and how he couldn't get it out of his mind.

"Sounds like she's making a big mistake." said Brendon.

"I think so too, but she is so confident about the protection the business promises, and her own abilities to stay safe, that she isn't going to listen to anyone else. Not even her best friend."

"Doesn't it seem weird to you that the only thing

standing between you and your dream girl is a little bit of money?"

"Now that you mention it, yes it does."

"And doesn't it seem even more weird to you that the only thing standing between ME and YOUR dream girl is a little bit of money?"

"Now that you mention it, *YES IT DOES*! You know, you're really not helping things any."

"Maybe not you, but I believe I'm helping me. I'm gonna have to think about this."

"Don't tell me *YOU* are considering it...I mean, you know, her!"

"I don't know. You are well aware I have zero social abilities when it comes to girls. My chances of getting a date are between slim and none...and I think slim has left town. On the other hand, I *DO* have money. Normally, the thought wouldn't even cross my mind, but since you know the girl, you've described her to me in great detail, and in a sense, told me what she would do to me, I am considering it."

"Dude! This is so out of character for you. Your Mr. play it safe, Mr. planning for the future, Mr. I don't think that would be prudent at this juncture. What gives?"

"Listen, I'm not perfect." Brendan's voice began to crack a little. "Everybody has their breaking point and I've been a pretty lonely guy my whole life. Yes, it's embarrassing to even entertain the thought of having to pay for it, but I would like to experience even a little bit of something like that. I'm lonely, inexperienced, and unconfident, but I have money. According to you, Zoe is the exact opposite of me. And didn't you say opposites attract? The whole reason this sort of thing has gone on for so long is because there will always be people like me and there will always be people like her."

"Okay man. I'm sorry. I'm not judging you; it just took me by surprise. I know you're a lonely guy. I also know you're a great guy and my best friend. And if this is going bring you happiness, then I say let it."

Aiden walked over to Brendan, arms wide. They both held back tears as they hugged each other. Brendan soon felt a little uncomfortable, so he let go and said, "Let's get back to work." They didn't speak much the rest of the day, only talking when it was about the roof they were building. Brendan wasn't one to let his feelings show and Aiden hated to see his friend sad. Also, the thought of Brendan and Zoe together, had Aiden feeling quite conflicted.

As soon as everything was all framed up, Aiden checked his phone and said, "Perfect timing!"

"You got plans tonight?"

"Yeah, just dinner at home with Amy." He didn't want to mention that Zoe was coming over and have another uncomfortable conversation.

"Alright man, thanks so much for helping me out. I

really appreciate it."

"For you, any time. Next Saturday, we do it again?"

"If you would be so kind sir."

"All right bud, I'll see you then... or maybe sooner!"

Aiden got back in time to get cleaned up before Zoe arrived, just like he promised. Amy was in a really good mood. She was so happy that Zoe was coming over. She was humming to herself as she set the table and then began singing everything she was doing, "Washing the carrots and peeling the carrots and chopping the carrots and boom-boom-boom! Oil in the pan and butter in the pan and salt and pepper and garlic bang-bang! Look at my boyfriend and go to my boyfriend and kissing my boyfriend kiss-kiss-kiss!"

"Someone's excited about company tonight."

"Oh, it's all I've been thinking about today. It seems like forever since I've seen Zoe and I've been so worried about her. Tonight, I don't have to worry. Tonight, I can just relax and enjoy spending time with my friend."

"That's great sweetie, I'm happy for you. Do you think it's time to put the steaks on?"

"Let's just wait till she-" Just then the doorbell rang. "Yes!"

Amy practically ran to the front door. She flung it open and wrapped Zoe in a hug. "It's so good to see you!"

She exclaimed. The two hugged and kissed until Aiden said, "How about bringing that action inside before you start drawing a crowd."

The girls held hands as they walked into the kitchen with Amy beaming at Zoe the whole way. Amy's smile was infectious and so Zoe began beaming back at her. Amy grabbed her up into her arms again, held her tight, and kissed her face.

Aiden raised his eyebrows as he slowly backed away and said, "Okay then, I guess I'll leave you two alone and go put the steaks on."

Amy took a bottle of wine out of the pantry. "Look, I got your favorite!"

Zoe laughed and reached into the bag she was holding. She pulled out Amy's favorite bottle of wine. "Great minds think alike!"

Taking out two long stemmed wine glasses, Amy began to sing again, "Hanging with my best friend and drinking with my best friend and loving on my best friend a bing-bang-boom!"

Mimicking Aiden's earlier exit, Zoe began to slowly back away and said, "I think I'll help Aiden with the steaks."

The two laughed. Amy opened the bottle and poured them each a healthy glass of wine. "Friends forever!" They said as they clinked their glasses together. The girls chatted happily as Amy made the finishing touches on dinner. Aiden opened the sliding glass door and poked his head into the living room,

"Steaks are ready when you are."

"Five minutes sweetie." Amy said, as steam billowed from the stove.

Soon everything was ready and the three sat down at the dinner table. Acting like the maître d' of a gourmet restaurant, Aiden described the meal using a comical French accent.

"For dinner tonight, we have a beautifully grilled Fillet Mignon, scalloped potatoes au Groton, pan seared snow peas in a garlic -butter sauce, and candied baby carrots. After the meal, you will have your choice from a number of delectable desserts from *A Taste of Europe*, our fine city's best pastry shop. Immediately following dessert, we will retire to the living room and continue to drink ourselves into a stupor! "

Everyone enjoyed their dinner. The conversation was lighthearted and fun, interspersed with sporadic sparring between Aiden and Zoe. As the two girls were engaged in conversation, Aiden found himself staring at Zoe. Somehow, she was even more beautiful than he remembered. Was it that his perception had changed, absence making the heart grow fonder, so to speak, or was it Zoe having money allowed her to get the best of everything: hairstyles, manicures, facials, makeup, tanning salons, perfume, sexy clothes... he didn't know, but he knew he liked what he saw. Without thinking about it, Aiden quietly said, "Am I dreaming right now?"

The conversation came to an abrupt halt with both girls turning to look at him. Zoe raised an eyebrow, tilted her head towards Aiden and looked at Amy as if to say, *"I think the boy is losing it."* Amy asked Aiden to explain, which he did, in great detail. Zoe seemed kind of intrigued by the idea.

"Well, let me give you something work with."

Zoe stood up, walked over to Aiden, and bent over at the waist, placing her hands on her knees. With her face just inches away from his, she gently swayed her shoulders making her breasts jiggle slightly as she looked Aiden in the eye and said in a breathy voice, "I hope you dream of me sweetie." And then blew him a kiss.

"Oh my gosh Zoe!" Amy said, stunned by her actions.

"You know how I love to tease the boy. I'm just having fun. I don't mean anything by it."

Wanting to change the subject, Amy stood up and said, "All right, let's move this party to another location."

The entertaining couple decided to forgo the washing of the dishes and prepared for round two in the living room. Aiden went into the kitchen to get a tumbler full of ice and a bottle of whiskey. Amy grabbed a couple of fresh wine glasses from the rack above the sink while Zoe opened the second bottle. Aiden's head was reeling as he walked to the living room. When Zoe was in his face, he could feel her warm, wine-laced breath on his lips. He could smell her perfume. He could see down her blouse, and hoped that Amy hadn't noticed. The three took their regular spots with Aiden sitting next to Amy on the sofa and Zoe in the chair across from them. Although they had been talking all night long, not a word was mentioned about Zoe's work. She knew Amy didn't want to hear about it, so she just didn't bring it up. Aiden however, was dying to hear about it. The curiosity was killing him. He thought maybe he could steer the conversation there, carefully, without it seeming obvious. He patiently waited until everyone seemed sufficiently inebriated before he started in.

"You still driving around on those old bologna skins?"

"If you're asking me, did I get new tires on my car, yes. In fact, I also got a brake job, new belts and hoses, and a killer stereo! And in case you were wondering, I've done a bunch of other things too: I've paid off all but one of my credit cards, I practically have an entire new wardrobe, and I am currently enrolled in college."

"Oh my gosh, Zoe, that is fantastic!" Amy said, slapping her hands on her knees with every syllable. "What are you studying?"

"Well, I thought about it for quite some time. If I'm going to choose a career, I want it to be something I would be good at and something I actually enjoy."

Aiden wanted to blurt out, "I thought you were already doing that," but he knew that would upset Amy, so he kept it to himself.

Zoe continued, "Then I thought to myself, I like being fit, I like working out, I mean, I'm at the gym almost every day as it is, so I've decided to become a personal trainer. The money is good, the hours are flexible, I get a free membership at the gym, and all the time I need to work out myself."

"That sounds perfect! I think you will be a great personal trainer." Amy was so happy to hear this news her eyes started welling up.

Sensing that Amy was on the edge of bursting into tears, Aiden took the spotlight off of her by saying, "I must admit, that's brilliant! Other girls will want you to train them because they want to look like you and guys will want you to train them just so they can be around you. Seriously, I don't think you'll have any trouble building up your clientele."

"Well, if it goes anything like my current line of work, I will be quite successful."

"What do you mean?" Aiden asked, although he was pretty sure he knew exactly what she meant.

"I know you don't want to talk about this Amy, but I honestly think if you hear me out, you will feel better about the situation. All the girls that work where I do make good money. I make *GREAT* money. When someone calls and says "Send a girl over" its 350 bucks, of which I get 250. When someone calls and says "Send so-and-so over." It's 500, of which I make 350. I've got to the point where every call I go on is a repeat customer who's asked for me by name and because they're all repeat customers, I know exactly what I'm getting into. I feel very safe. Which brings us to tonight: On my way over here, I got a call from work. Someone asked for me by name, but I've never met them before. He said he was referred by a friend. I'm getting word-of-mouth customers asking for me by name and paying top dollar for me. My pussy is a gold mine!"

"Zoe!" Amy buried her face in her hands. With a muffled voice she asked, "How is that supposed to make me feel better?"

"Sorry, I got carried away. The point is, I have made so much more money, so much more quickly than I thought I would, that I'll be able to quit in about a month. I just want to pay off my last credit card and put enough money into savings to carry me through school. Then I can start over, debt free, with a real job. And then, you won't have to worry about me anymore and I will have all sorts of time to spend with you."

Amy began to cry. Zoe didn't know if they were tears of relief, or joy, or continuing sadness. Zoe stood up and gently took Amy's hands. She pulled her to her feet and wrapped her arms around her. The girls embraced and quietly whispered in each other's ears. Zoe was comforting Amy and Amy was encouraging Zoe. Aiden just sat there, staring into space. His mind was racing, *"The first-timer who called and asked for Zoe by name, could it be Brendan? Am I the friend who referred him? I can't believe this is happening."* The thought of Brendan and Zoe together filled Aiden with such conflicting emotions. He was happy for Brendan. He felt bad for Brendan. He envied Brendan. He felt resentment, remorse, and anger towards himself... It was too much! He began to feel self-conscious, that the girls would notice his emotional state. He turned and looked at them, still hugging, still whispering, like he wasn't even there. He took the opportunity to get up and walk out of the room.

"I'm going to put the grill up." He said as he grabbed his tumbler of whiskey and stepped outside.

Aiden stood on the patio staring at the moon. He took a deep breath and let it go, followed by a sip of whiskey. He repeated this over and over until his glass was empty. Then he just stood there, not moving a muscle. He didn't know what to think. He didn't know how to feel. After about 15 minutes, the sliding glass door opened. Aiden turned around to see Zoe coming out.

"Hey Aiden, I didn't forget about you." She pulled two bottles out of her purse and set them on the little plastic table by the grill. "One is Xanax, just like before. The other is Lunesta. It works differently. I thought maybe you might want to try it to see if it's any better."

Aiden was surprised how Zoe seemed to go out of her way for him. He also wondered how she was getting the stuff, but he knew better than to ask again.

"Wow that's great!   Thanks again Zoe, I really appreciate it."

"Don't mention it...and I appreciate the referral." She leaned in and gave him a kiss on the cheek.

Aiden stood there with his mouth hanging open. He couldn't move. He couldn't speak. He couldn't believe she knew.

"Don't worry, I won't tell Amy a thing." She smiled and winked, then turned and walked away.

Aiden watched Amy through the sliding glass door as she saw Zoe out. He shook his head quickly side to side and said to himself, "Come on, pull your shit together." He quickly closed the grill, put the cover on, and rolled it up against the apartment building. Remembering the pills, he grabbed the bottles and stuffed them into his pocket. Just then, Amy stepped outside, still looking weepy, and came to Aiden for comfort. Aiden put his hands on her shoulders and said,

"Come on now, it really was a good night."

"Yeah, right up until the last few minutes, and then..." Amy gestured an explosion with her hands.

"If you think about it, even the last five minutes were good. She told you all the good things she's been able to do with her money, she told you that she's enrolled in college, she told you she has an excellent plan for a career, and she told you a month from now she will be done with all of this."

"I guess you're right, but as long as I know she's still doing...that, I'm going to worry about her."

"I know you are, because you are her best friend and you care about her. Listen, why don't you go ahead and get ready for bed. I'll clean up the kitchen and join you as soon as I'm done."

Amy forced a small, tight lipped, smile and slowly nodded her head. The two walked into the apartment with Aiden locking the sliding glass door behind them and drawing the blinds. Amy sulked into the bedroom as Aiden got to work cleaning up the kitchen. Once he had finished, he started for the bedroom but then remembered the pills in his pocket. No amount of binaural beats or meditation was going to get him to sleep tonight. He popped one of each of the pills into his mouth and slurped water out of the kitchen faucet. By the time he got into the bedroom, Amy was fast asleep. It gave him relief to see her lying there so peacefully. Her suffering was over for the night, but he felt like his was just beginning.

6 Deep Cut

Aiden laid in bed, on his back, staring at the ceiling. Considering when Zoe left and what time it was now, he could only imagine that she was at Brendan's house at that very moment. He had trouble getting her out of his mind before, but this was ridiculous. Every time he tried to think about something else, a moment later, it was back to Zoe. It wouldn't be long until the pills began to take effect, so he decided to focus all the more on her, hoping to at least see her in his dreams. He thought about what Zoe had done earlier that night, getting in his face, and what she said to him. He thought about it over and over and over again. Sleep crept up slowly on him, wrapped his body in a soothing, warm, fuzzy, feeling and took him.

Hours later, Aiden's phone began vibrating across the nightstand. He answered in a groggy voice, " Hello, who is it?" It was Brendan, asking him to come over right away. He sounded upset. Aiden got up, threw on some clothes, grabbed his keys, and scribbled a quick note for Amy before leaving. At this time of night, traffic was nonexistent and he got to Brendan's house in record time. Pulling up to the house, Aiden noticed just a few lights on inside. As he walked up to the front door, it flew open.

"I'm so glad you're here. Zoe's inside and I thought maybe you could help me."

"You know I'm always willing to help you buddy, but what is it you want me to do?"

"I don't know. She's just too much for me. She's so beautiful, and so aggressive, it's intimidating. Come on."

Aiden followed Brendan into his bedroom to find Zoe bare naked, laying on the bed, legs spread wide and touching herself. When she saw Aiden, she gasped and grabbed for the sheets to cover up.

"What are *YOU* doing here?!"

"My buddy called and said he needed help, so here I am."

"And how is it you expect to help?"

"I'm not sure."

Brenden spoke up," Maybe I could just watch this first time."

"Dude! You want to watch *US*?" Aiden said, pointing

back and forth between himself and Zoe.

Zoe spoke up, "I don't think I can do this. I have no problem doing you, but Amy is my best friend and I can't do this to her."

Aiden looked at Brendan. Then he looked at Zoe. "Am I dreaming right now?"

Neither of them said a word. Aiden looked at the clock, it was 1:43. Brendan walked up to the edge of the bed and grabbed hold of the sheets. He started to tug at them but Zoe frantically pulled them back. Aiden tried to look at the clock again, but in the ensuing struggle, Zoe had knocked it off of the nightstand. The two fought over the sheets a while until Brendan was able to wrestle them away from Zoe.

"Look, I paid 500 bucks for you. You had no idea who I was, so what does it matter who you fuck?"

"I knew it wasn't *HIM*!" Zoe said, motioning to Aiden.

Brenden turned to Aiden, "Come on man let's go!" with obvious agitation in his voice.

Aiden had never heard Brendan sound like this before. *"There's no way this is real."* Aiden stripped off his clothes as fast as he could and climbed on top of Zoe.

"Don't do this Aiden!" Zoe said through her gritted teeth.

"Look, I promise I won't tell Amy a thing." Aiden said

with a smile and a wink.

"Okay, I think you have the situation under control." Brendan said as he sat down in a chair in the corner of the room.

For the next 10 minutes, Aiden did whatever he wanted. Zoe never stopped staring into his eyes, wrath burning in her gaze, but she did not resist. Just as Aiden was about to cum, he gasped, heart pounding, sweating, laying in his bed next to Amy. Another lucid dream.

Aiden thought to himself, *"Wow, that Lunesta is something else! Even when I knew it was a dream, I could still stay asleep. That was fucking amazing!"*

The next week was one of the longest for Aiden. He couldn't wait until Saturday morning when he would see Brendan and hopefully find out about Zoe. All day long, whether he was working in the office or in the field, he mulled it over in his mind again and again. He tried to think of a way to make everything all right, a way that he could look at things and have some peace about the situation, but he never reached that place. Nighttime wasn't any better. One Xanax wasn't doing it anymore, it was always two now, along with a Lunesta. He thought about Zoe every night as he lay awake in bed, waiting for sleep to take him, but he never dreamt of her. He dreamt about the girl who worked at the bookstore. He dreamed about Brendan. He dreamt about having a mouth full of leaves, that no matter how many he pulled out, there was still too many to speak. He didn't know if it was because of the increase in Xanax, or the Lunesta, but his dreams became so much more vivid and so much stranger.

When Aiden woke up Saturday morning, he laid in bed a while, still feeling groggy from staying up so late with Amy the previous night. They were drinking and playing "guilty pleasures". It was something they would do from time to time: taking turns playing songs on YouTube that they really liked but were embarrassed to admit to anyone that they did. After one would pick a song, the other would either admit their love for the song or pass judgment in the most brutal fashion possible. They both found it to be quite entertaining. Suddenly, Aiden shook like he had been shocked and whispered to himself, "Saturday morning, I need to get to Brendan's house!" He got out of bed, threw on some work clothes, grabbed a protein bar from the kitchen cabinet and a sports drink from the fridge, then bolted out the door. As he was driving, he felt a little sick to his stomach, as if he was click-clacking slowly up the rails at the beginning of a rollercoaster ride. He wanted to talk to Brendan about Zoe... and he didn't. After a week of suffering over the situation, he knew he had to bring it up. He also knew that he would NOT tell Brendan about his dream. Pulling up to the house, he found Brendan already outside, taking materials out of the garage and laying them out for the day's work. Brendan waved and gave a friendly smile as Aiden parked the car.

Aiden hopped out of the car and stood at attention, giving his best Benny Hill salute. "Private Aiden reporting for duty Sir."

"At ease private, who obviously tests helmets for grenade resistance."

Laughing, the two greeted each other with a handshake and a smile. Brendan motioned for Aiden to grab the other end of a sheet of plywood. They picked it up and started walking around the house to the backyard.

"So, how's your week been?" Aiden asked.

"Fair to midland, not too much excitement. How about you?"

"Kind of rough actually, had a lot on my mind and sleep doesn't come easy, well, not without professional strength help."

"Sorry to hear that buddy. Anything I can do?"

"I don't know. For some reason, I just can't get Zoe out of my mind. It's becoming a problem. You know, all the things we're talking about last weekend."

"Well, I don't think this is going to help you any", Brendan said, "but I actually made a call and she's coming over tonight for what I hope is going to be an awesome experience."

"Are you serious?" Aiden said, trying his best to act surprised. At the same time, strangely enough, he felt somewhat relieved that he hadn't seen her already. Maybe he thought somehow he would talk Brendan out of it or he would chicken out at the last minute and call it off. Brendan could tell something was going on with Aiden, making him uncomfortable, so he made a suggestion:

"Listen, last time we were talking about her, things didn't go so well. How about we just leave that topic alone for today."

"Okay man, if that's what you want."

Aiden's heart sunk into his stomach. Now there was no talking him out of it. And if the subject was taboo, he couldn't even get the details to satisfy his curiosity. He knew he was going to have to find a way to deal with this, but he didn't know how yet. Brendan quickly changed the subject and did his best to take both their minds off of Zoe. Aiden could see that Brendan was making an effort to make them both more comfortable and so he did his best to appreciate it. When it was time to break for lunch, Brendan treated to Thai food delivery, Aiden's favorite local brew, and a hazelnut praline cheesecake he had bought the night before. The mood felt lighter and the two exchanged funny stories about jobs they had while they were teenagers while they ate. After lunch, they went back to work, figuring they had quite a way yet to go. It was almost dusk when they finished. They got all the plywood up and the shingles on just in time, as a thunderstorm formed in the distance. It was obvious rain was on the way, so they hurried to clean up before it got there. All the wood scraps went into a couple of metal trash cans that Brendan used to hold kindling for the wood stove. They made sure to pick up all the bent nails that they had thrown down while finishing the roof. Brendan bent over to pick up the reciprocating saw. As he stood up, he accidentally stepped on the cord, which ripped the saw out of his hand.

"Mother fucker!" Brendan screamed. The blade of the saw had sliced his hand open, deep. Aiden rushed over to help him.

"Dude, that looks bad! That's going to need stitches in a big way." Aiden said.

"I think you're right. Help me get it wrapped up." The two rushed into the house and gathered up some gauze pads and tape. Aiden wrapped it up tight as Brendan winced in pain.

"All right, let's get you to the ER." Aiden said.

"No, I can drive myself. This isn't life-threatening. Who knows how long I am going to have to wait there? Please just finish putting everything away and lock the house up for me."

"Are you sure? I could drop you off then come back and clean up."

"I'll be fine...and I don't like the thought of leaving everything out in the storm. Put everything away and button this place up, OK?"

"You got it. Just send me a text when you get to the hospital to let me know you got there."

"Will do."

Brendan got into his car and took off for the hospital. Aiden hustled to get everything picked up before the storm hit. The wind was picking up and Aiden could smell the rain in the air. "Looks like this one is going to be a humdinger." Aiden said to himself. Flashes of lightning lit up the sky as thunder rumbled low and ominous. Just as Aiden was putting the last of the tools away, the sky opened up. He rushed through the house, closing all the windows to keep the rain from pouring in. It was raining so hard, Aiden decided to wait it out a while to see if it would let up. Aiden's phone chimed, and when he checked it, he saw that Brendan had made it to the hospital all right. He texted back, *"Hope everything is okay. Let me know if there's anything I can do for you."* Then, he texted Amy to tell her what had happened and that he would be home later. Amy texted back saying she got a last-minute invite and went to meet a few people from work at a bar downtown for drinks and appetizers and not to wait up. Aiden relaxed on the couch, watching the storm through the bay window of the living room. After a hard day's work and the adrenaline dump from Brendan's injury, the sound of the rain beating on the roof lulled Aiden to sleep.

7 Too Much

Thump, thump, thump! "What the hell?" Aiden mumbled to himself. "How long have I been sleeping?" Thump, thump, thump! Someone was at the door. Aiden thought, *"Maybe it's Brendan coming back from the hospital. If his hand is all stitched up, he may have trouble putting the key in the lock."* Aiden got up and went to the front door. When he slung it open, there stood Zoe.

Zoe's eyes bulged as she said, "What the hell are *YOU* doing here?"

"Come on in, you're soaking wet."

Aiden opened the door wide and motioned her in. Lightning flashed and a loud clap of thunder followed just after. Zoe shrieked and jumped into the house with Aiden closing the door behind her.

"Brendan's not here. We were working out back and

he cut his hand with a saw. He went to the ER to get stitched up. I don't know when he'll be back."

"So, you are here waiting for me?"

"With all the excitement, Brendan getting hurt and the storm, I forgot about you coming over. I bet Brendan did too. He was trying to act like it was no big deal, but the dude was pale as a sheet. I was just waiting out the storm and fell asleep. I don't want to drive around in this if I don't have to."

"Tell me about it. The streets are flooded, some traffic signals are out, and I hate being out when it's lightning."

"Well, you can hang out here with me until the storm lets up. Hold on a sec." Aiden turned and walked out of the room, coming back moments later with a couple of towels.

"Here you go, get yourself dried off while I see what old Brendan has in the liquor cabinet."

He spun around and headed towards the bookshelf in the corner of the living room. Swinging open the doors on the top shelf, he perused the libations.

"Rats, no whiskey. I guess gin will have to do."

He grabbed the bottle and disappeared around the corner. Zoe could hear all sorts of noises coming from the kitchen: cabinet doors opening and closing, drawers sliding in and out, the refrigerator door being opened and closed, water running from the sink, the sounds of a knife on a cutting board, and ice cubes clinking in glasses. Aiden returned with some nicely made gin and tonics, complete with a fresh lime wedge. He handed Zoe a glass and held his up, "Salute!"

The two clinked their glasses together and took a sip. Aiden plopped down on the couch and Zoe sat next to him.

"Well, this is not quite what I had planned for the evening." Zoe said sarcastically.

"Me neither, but shit happens and you just got a roll with it. I always try to make the best of every situation." Aiden said as he took another sip of his drink followed by a loud, "Ahhh!"

"Yeah, I guess you're right." Zoe said, mimicking Aiden's sipping and following noises.

The drinks were soon gone and Aiden said, "All right, let's do it again."

He grabbed both glasses and headed back to the kitchen. Zoe stood up and walked over to the mirror to check her look.

"Oh my God, I'm a wreck." she said, as she began to comb her hair with her fingers, straighten her shirt collar, and do a little makeup maintenance.

Walking back into the room with another round of drinks, Aiden said, "Don't worry about it, it's just me. Besides, you are incapable of looking anything but hot."

"Well, thank you for your support." She said with a pleasant smile.

"Don't mention it. I always say, if the truth hurts, wear it...or something like that."

The two went back to their seats on the couch and clinked their glasses together again, "Salute!"

They drank and chatted until the drinks were gone. At that point, Zoe kicked off her shoes and put her feet up on the coffee table in front of them. She slid down in her seat so that her head rested on the back rest of the couch.

"I don't know what I'm supposed to do right now. Brendan's already paid, but I don't know when he will be back or how long I should wait for him. He was the last stop for the night. I could probably just go home, but it's still coming down pretty hard out there. I'd like to wait it out a little longer if I could. "

"I've got nowhere to go and nothing to do. Amy is out with friends and told me not to wait up, so she won't be home 'till the wee hours me thinkst. Stay as long as you like."

Aiden couldn't be happier. He wanted Zoe to stay. After thinking about her all week and not being able to say a word about her, now he was saying words *TO* her. He found just being in her presence was exhilarating. He had never been alone with Zoe before. Amy was always there. Zoe was so laid-back, friendly, and comfortable with herself; she just drew you in.

"Be right back." Aiden said, picking up the glasses.

"Round three?"

"Round three!"

Returning with the next round, he handed Zoe her drink and said, "Another clink, another drink."

Zoe took a sip. "Whew, That's a stiff one!"

"That's what she said."

Zoe chuckled and shook her head, then took another sip. Aiden downed his drink in one go. "Ahhhh!" Aiden could feel the alcohol was kicking in. He could sense that Zoe was feeling it too.

Looking out the window at the storm, Zoe seemed to mentally shift gears and said, "You know what? It's kind of nice to have the rest of the night off".

She sat up, untucked her shirt and lay down on the couch with her feet in Aiden's lap. Aiden thought to himself, *"I'm not a foot person, but damn, even her feet are pretty!"* He wanted to touch her so badly that he couldn't stand it. He took one of her feet into his hands and began to give her a gentle foot massage. Zoe closed her eyes and draped her hands behind her head so they hung off the end of the couch.

She arched her back and purred," Oh, that feels so

good. Walking around in four-inch pumps is not conducive to happy feet."

Aiden switched back and forth between her feet, massaging them, gently rubbing them, lightly tickling them with his fingertips. He looked down at Zoe. She was so beautiful, so perfect, so sexy. He slid his hands up to her calves, lightly running his fingers across her skin. Zoe got goosebumps. For a moment, as she slid down the couch towards him so he could reach her more easily, Aiden got a glimpse up her short black leather skirt. He saw she was not wearing any panties. It was too much for him. He scooted towards her and ran his fingers gently up the inside of her lower legs, past her knees, and up her thighs.

"Aiden, what are you doing?"

"Zoe, I have to admit, I think about you all the time. Now that the two of us are alone and both feeling a bit loosened up, I find you absolutely irresistible."

"I understand where you're coming from sweetie, but it's not going to happen."

"Listen, I have an idea. How about you and I get together tonight and when I see Brendan, I'll pay him what he paid you. You'll get what you came here for, I'll get what I want so badly, and Brendan isn't out a dime. Just this once. We don't have to tell Amy a thing. "

"Counter offer. If you can get Amy to agree to it, then I'm good to go. You're a fine-looking piece of machinery yourself and I'd be all about it."

Hearing this just stoked Aiden's fire more. Knowing that Zoe found him attractive and wanted to fuck him made him feel that much closer to making it happen "Zoe please. You know what I think about sex. It has nothing to do with my love for Amy. It would only be physical. It's just fucking."

"I know that's what you think and I am right there with you, but that's not where *SHE* is at and that's what throws a wrench in the works. I can't see how telling her it's only physical would make her feel any better about it." Zoe's tone suddenly shifted. With an undeniable bite she said, " It would undoubtedly damage, if not completely destroy, our friendship and one fuck just isn't worth it."

Zoe swung around and put her feet on the floor. She bent over and started putting her shoes back on. Aiden apologized and begged her not to leave, but she continued to gather her things without saying a word. As she headed for the door, Aiden darted in front of her, and put his hand up against it.

"Get out of my way."

"Please don't go."

Zoe glared at Aiden and said through gritted teeth, "Move, now!"

"No, listen to me, I just want to talk-"

Zoe was not one to be told what to do or to be held

against her will. She reared her right foot back and kneed Aiden in the crotch. Aiden dropped to his hands and knees and groaned. Zoe grabbed the door and yanked it open, pushing Aiden out of the way with it. She made just enough room to squeeze through. Running through the rain, she jumped into her car, fired it up, and sped off. By the time Aiden picked himself up off the ground, she was long gone. "Dammit!" he slammed the door shut. He slowly walked through the house, still hurting from the blow, straightening up the place. Once he had finished cleaning up in the kitchen, he grabbed his things, turned off the lights and left.

On the way home, Aiden began berating himself, "You stupid fuck! What the hell were you thinking? You're thinking with the wrong head is what you're thinking. What are you gonna do now? Now Zoe hates you and you will *NEVER* touch her. How are you going to un-fuck this?" He then focused his anger on Zoe, "...and what the fuck is wrong with that crazy bitch? All I wanted to do was talk to her before she left, try to explain myself a little better. So, she knees me in the fucking balls! That was totally uncalled for, totally unnecessary!"

With all of the rain, standing water in the street, and flashing lights at the intersections, it took Aiden twice as long to get home as it took for him to get to Brendan's. Arriving back at the apartment, he jumped out of the car, slammed the door, and ran through the pouring rain all the way to the front door. He fumbled for the key in the dark, but finally managed to get the door open. Aiden just kept replaying the events of the evening over and over in his head. Throwing his hands up in the air, he said, "Well, I guess there's nothing I can do about it now."

After peeling off all of his wet clothes, Aiden grabbed his T-shirt and boxers from under the pillow and got dressed for bed. He opened up the nightstand drawer and pulled the two pill bottles out. Two Lunesta, three Xanax, and a few gulps of water from the bathroom faucet, then Aiden dragged himself into the living room and flopped down onto the couch. He turned on the TV, and waited for sleep to take him.

After all the hard work at Brendan's, the stress of dealing with his injury, the blowup with Zoe, and the raging storm, Aiden was wiped out. The pills worked their magic in record time, and soon he slipped off to a deep sleep. It was only a short while later, Aiden began to dream of Zoe. She was kneeling by the couch, gently calling his name. When he turned his head to look at her, he saw she was wearing a white, wife beater T-shirt, cut off jean shorts, and sneakers with no socks. She asked,

"Is it all right if I sit next to you on the couch? We can talk."

Aiden looked at the clock on the living room wall,12:47. He slowly got up off the couch and looked through the pass-through into the kitchen to see the clock on the stove, 4:39. "That's it, dreamtime!" Just as Zoe was about to sit down on the couch, Aiden grabbed her up in his arms and pulled her tight up against himself. He leaned in and began kissing her mouth, his tongue thrusting between her lips. Zoe pushed back. Aiden slipped his leg behind her so she couldn't catch herself and pushed her backwards, tripping her and then gently lowering her to the floor. He laid down on the floor beside her. He slid his hand up Zoe's shirt and grabbed her breast.

"No bra, how convenient." He said with a grin.

"Please don't Aiden, I just wanted to talk."

Aiden slid off his boxers. He then began to work on Zoe's shorts, unbuttoning and unzipping them with one hand while holding Zoe down with the other.

"Impressed?" He asked. Zoe didn't answer him. He slid them off and said, "No panties, how convenient."

Aiden began rubbing Zoe's clit with his thumb while slipping his fingers in and out of her pussy. She began to push him away with more urgency. Aiden rolled on top of her, and pried her legs apart, slipping in between them. He reached down and grabbed himself in order to maneuver inside of her. Zoe put her hand on his chest and said,

"Please, not that, okay?"

Aiden shook his head and said, "Not in *MY* dream." Aiden thrust himself into her.

"Aiden!" Zoe shouted.

Aiden put his hand over her mouth. He pushed deeper and harder and faster. Zoe tried to bite his hand, so he grabbed her by the throat and squeezed her neck. Zoe let out a scream so Aiden put his palm under her chin and pushed hard, forcing her mouth shut. He kept pushing until her neck was stretched out as far as it could go, her head facing the wall behind her. A mixture of tears and mascara made trails down her face. Zoe was strong, and did her best to struggle free, but she was no match for Aiden. He took his other hand and wrapped it around her throat,

"...and *THIS* is for kneeing me in the balls!"

He began to squeeze as hard as he could. Zoe squirmed all the more. She kicked her legs and flailed her arms to no avail. She tried punching and slapping Aiden wherever she could, but he just squeezed harder and harder. Zoe's arms fell limp to the ground beside her. Her legs flopped open. Blood trickled out of her nose and frothy spit dripped from her mouth. Just then, Aiden came. "Finally, I get to finish before waking up." Just as he was getting up off of her, he heard a bloodcurdling scream. He looked up to see Amy looking like she was going into shock.

"Aiden, what did you do?" She pointed at Zoe laying on the ground.

"It's okay sweetie, this is just a dream. When I wake up, everything will be fine."

"Oh my God, Aiden, no!" Amy dropped to her knees and cradled Zoe's head in her hands.

"I hate to see you like this Amy." Aiden began repeating to himself, "I want to wake up now, I want to wake up now, I want to wake up now!"

"Aiden, this is *NOT* a dream. This is *REAL*!"

Aiden began slapping himself. He ran into the kitchen and flushed his face with water. Lightning struck and the lights flickered. The apartment rumbled with the thunder. He looked at the clock on the stove,12:00. "I want to wake up, I want to wake up!"

Epilogue:

Aiden lay in his bed, heart pounding and dripping with sweat. He ran his fingers through his long, thick, brown, curly hair and then rubbed his face, "When is this nightmare ever going to end?"

"For you, it's gonna end in 10 to 20, depending on your behavior." His cellmate quipped, "Now shut the fuck up and let me sleep!"

Aiden could hear screams reverberating through the cellblock. His bed was uncomfortable. His new orange jumpsuit was stiff and scratchy. He had hardly slept a wink since he started serving his sentence. Because of the circumstances involving the drugs he was taking, Aiden was able to plea down to manslaughter.

Zoe went home that night. As she was lying in her bed, she kept playing the events of the evening over and over in her mind. She felt bad about hurting Aiden. He did say he just wanted to talk. She decided to quickly get dressed and go to the apartment to apologize to him. When she arrived, she could see the TV was on through the living room window. When he didn't answer the door, she let herself in with the key they had hidden in a fake rock in the bushes. She had seen Amy use it once before. The clock on the living room wall was battery powered. The clock on the stove was not. The lightning from the storm caused the lights to flicker and threw the stove clock off. Because Aiden didn't have a prescription for the Lunesta he was taking, he didn't know of the possible side effects listed in the accompanying literature: Sleepwalking, eating while asleep, driving while asleep, and even having sex while still being asleep. The more he used it and Xanax together, the harder it became to distinguish when he was awake or dreaming. After Zoe's funeral, Amy quit her job at the zoo, sold all of her personal belongings, and joined a group that was doing humanitarian work in Haiti. After serving just six weeks in prison, Aiden killed himself by leaping over the third story railing, headfirst, down to the main floor below.

8 ALTERNATE ENDING #1

Epilogue:

Aiden lay in his bed, heart pounding and dripping with sweat. He ran his fingers through his long, thick, brown, curly hair and then rubbed his face. He looked up at the ceiling and saw drop panels and florescent lights. He looked at the bed, covered with white sheets and surrounded by metal rails. He heard beeps and chimes. There were wires and tubes attached to him. He felt groggy, dizzy, disoriented.

"Where the hell am I?" Aiden said in a quiet, scratchy, voice.

He heard a scuffling in the room, which startled him. He gasped!

"It's OK sweetie, it's OK. We're here, everybody's here.

Aiden looked up to see Amy, Brendan, … and Zoe! "Oh my gosh, you're alive!", Aiden said reaching out to Zoe. "I'm so sorry, I'm so sorry."

The three of them looked at Aiden, puzzled.

"Of course *I'M* alive, it's *YOU* we were worried about. What are you talking about?"

"I thought I killed you. I thought you saw me do it," Aiden said, motioning to Amy. "It must have been another bad dream. What happened? Why am I in the hospital?"

Amy took Aiden's hand and caressed it. Tears began welling up in her eyes. "I came home last night and you were asleep on the couch. You're usually such a light sleeper, I thought it was odd you didn't wake up when I came in…and the way you were sleeping didn't look very comfortable, so I tried to wake you up to get you into bed…but you wouldn't wake up…you wouldn't wake up. I was terrified. I called 911. The ambulance came and when they couldn't revive you, they brought you here. I told them about the Xanax and Lunesta. They pumped you stomach, put some sort of charcoal in there, and hooked up an IV to flush everything out. I called Brendan and Zoe to come and wait with me. I was so worried about you. I don't know what I would do if I lost you. You're my everything."

"Holy shit, I really fucked up." Still talking to Amy, Aiden turned and looked at Zoe, "You have no idea how bad I fucked up."

Zoe gave Aiden a comforting look, and almost imperceptibly, slowly shook her head, as if to say, *"Water under the bridge. Don't worry about it. It will be our secret."*

Aiden lied there motionless. He stared off into space, thinking about what had happened, about Amy and Zoe, and about what *COULD* have happened. He thought about all he had, all he wanted, and all he might have lost. Aiden thought about the possibility of leaving Amy alone. He thought about his bad dreams and insomnia...and about what his mom had said. He thought about the drugs he was taking and his obsession with Zoe. He knew he was heading for trouble, but hadn't realized just how bad or forthcoming the trouble would be. He could one day kill someone, not being able to discern reality from a dream. Maybe the supposed freedom of what he allowed himself to think and do in his dreams *COULD* have real consequences..."*First you think it, then you do it*". He turned back to Amy, "I'm so sorry. I promise, I will never use those pills again...and I hope I never feel the need to. Finding you is the best thing that has ever happened to me. Losing you, would be the worst. If I ever thought of doing such a thing, this is not how I pictured it going down, but, I love you Amy and want to be with you for the rest of my life. Will you marry me?"

Without hesitation, Amy said, "I would love to!" and wrapped Aiden up in a hug.

"You made that way to easy sister. I would have let him stew at least a little while," Zoe said with a grin.

"Congratulations, I'm so happy for both of you," Brendan said, putting his hand on each of their shoulders...then quickly pulling his injured hand away, "Ouch!"

Aiden and Amy were married a few months later, in the woods, at the very spot where they first met. Zoe was the maid of honor (which Aiden made numerous jokes about) and Brendan was the best man. Zoe went on to get certified as a personal trainer and Brendan was one of her first clients. He later helped her open her own gym. The four remain friends to this day.

9 ALTERNATE ENDING #2

Epilogue:

Aiden lay in his bed, heart pounding and dripping with sweat. He ran his fingers through his long, thick, brown, curly hair and then rubbed his face. He looked up at the ceiling and saw drop panels and florescent lights. He looked at the bed, covered with white sheets and surrounded by metal rails. He heard beeps and chimes. There were wires and tubes attached to him. He felt groggy, dizzy, disoriented.

"Where the hell am I?" Aiden said in a quiet, scratchy, voice.

He heard a scuffling in the room, which startled him. He gasped!

"It's OK sweetie, it's OK.   We're here, everybody's here.

Aiden looked up to see Amy, Brendan, … and Zoe! "Oh my gosh, you're alive!", Aiden said reaching out to Zoe. "I'm so sorry, I'm so sorry."

The three of them looked at Aiden, puzzled.

"Of course *I'M* alive, it's *YOU* we were worried about. What are you talking about?"

"I thought I killed you. I thought you saw me do it," Aiden said, motioning to Amy. "It must have been another bad dream. What happened? Why am I in the hospital?"

Zoe explained, "I came over to Brendan's house and found you laying in the yard in the pouring rain. You were out! I figured if a cold shower wouldn't wake you, there wasn't anything I could do to help, so I called 911. The ambulance came and took you to the hospital. I called Amy and Brendan and let them know what was going on. Amy met me at the hospital and Brendan was already here. After they examined you in the ER, they figured out you had been struck by lightning!"

"I was struck by lightning?!"

"Shocking, isn't it!" Zoe quipped.

Aiden looked disgustedly at Zoe. Amy slowly shook her head. Brendan tried to hide a smirk.

"Too soon?"

"Yes!" the three of them said in unison.

Zoe continued, "They don't think it was a direct hit, or you'd be fried, but definitely close enough to jack you up with a fierceness."

Amy took Aiden's hand, kissed it, and held it to her face. "I was so worried about you. I don't know what I would do if I lost you. You're my everything."

Aiden lied there motionless. He stared off into space, thinking about what had happened, about Amy and Zoe, and about what *COULD* have happened. He thought about all he had, all he wanted, and all he might have lost. Aiden thought about the possibility of leaving Amy alone. He thought about his bad dreams and insomnia...and about what his mom had said. He thought about the drugs he was taking and his obsession with Zoe. He knew he was heading for trouble, but hadn't realized just how bad or forthcoming the trouble would be. He could one day kill someone, not being able to discern reality from a dream. Maybe the supposed freedom of what he allowed himself to think and do in his dreams *COULD* have real consequences..."*First you think it, then you do it*". He turned back to Amy, "I'm so sorry. I promise, I will never use those pills again...and I hope I never feel the need to. Finding you is the best thing that has ever happened to me. Losing you, would be the worst. If I ever thought of doing such a thing, this is not how I pictured it going down, but, I love you Amy and want to be with you for the rest of my life. Will you marry me?"

Without hesitation, Amy said, "I would love to!" and wrapped Aiden up in a hug.

"You made that way to easy sister. I would have let him stew at least a little while," Zoe said with a grin.

"Congratulations, I'm so happy for both of you," Brendan said, putting his hand on each of their shoulders...then quickly pulling his injured hand away, "Ouch!"

Aiden and Amy were married a few months later, in the woods, at the very spot where they first met. Zoe was the maid of honor (which Aiden made numerous jokes about) and Brendan was the best man. Zoe went on to get certified as a personal trainer and Brendan was one of her first clients. He later helped her open her own gym. The four remain friends to this day.

ABOUT THE AUTHOR

Robert J. L. Kun has an insatiable desire to create. He writes and records original music in his home studio, designs computer drawn artwork, writes poetry, performs stand-up comedy at local open-mic events, and produces videos for his YouTube channel. These artistic pursuits build upon one another to create a never-ending source of inspiration. This abundance of inspiration is clearly evident in his latest endeavor, writing the novella LUCID, which he describes as, "The intriguing process of combining the depth of the emotional experiences of my own life with copious amounts of imagination!"